Scandal

Lake

To Erin,

Hope you enjoy these tales of the lake. I can see you in the TV episodes for sure. Lots of love.

Adrienne Snyr

Dive in + enjoy!

Beth Liberty

Scandal Lake

Liberty Smyth

anticipated enthusiasm. Patty arrived as expected screeching into the driveway in her new Dodge Charger.

"How the heck are you?" she greeted her enthusiastically.

"Oh my god, I have been waiting so long for you to get here. Did your GPS give out, or your phone die?" Amy retorted teasingly.

It was an on-going joke that both often got lost on trips due to inadequate phone service, drained phone batteries, or some other task that forced them off the beaten track and inevitably delayed their arrival. Neither one minded any delay. They just rolled with it. Time was not a problem to them, but other people had issues with their disrespectful timekeeping and mutual tardiness. No need to be stressed with navigational issues, Patty and Amy just enjoyed the scenery and eventually got to their destination and to hell with the others waiting for them.

"You want to get something to eat, Patty?" Amy asked.

"Sure thing, get me some grits or whatever they serve up here in the boonies. I saw a guy with a dead racoon slung over his back, blood dripping down his naked torso, walking along the road, on the way here. Perhaps we could get some barbeque racoon locally?" She laughed vociferously.

"Sure thing Miss Patty, we can get that right up for you," she retorted in a local drawl and they merrily headed out for dinner.

The local restaurants left a lot to be desired, but one couldn't go wrong with a hamburger at least. They went to the nearest greasy spoon, where they ordered two burgers. When the meal was served, Patty's looked fine, but Amy's was a little light on the French fries.

"Excuse me," Amy asked the waitress, "is there a potato famine here?" She pointed to the measly 4 pieces of overcooked potato strips on the plate and scowled at the waitress.

"Oh, do you want some more? I'll be right back." The waitress moved quickly away from the table, to the kitchen cursing the women under her breath.

"What the fuck?" Amy demanded of Patty who laughed back at her.

"You're a waitress's nightmare!" Patty exclaimed and offered her some fries.

The waitress returned with a huge plate of fries, too hot to eat and Amy began to relax immediately.

"OK, maybe I'll tip her now." Her merry mood returned.

The cousins finished their meals of burgers and fries and set off back to the lake house.

"You want to check out the local dive bar? Maybe your racoon guy will be there?" She giggled mischievously.

"Why the hell not? Let's see what's going on. Gotta be some fun somewhere," Patty replied.

"Let's boogie! It might be good to get to know some locals, blue-collar, hard-working, and fun-loving people. To the local dive bar then!" They jumped into the car.

Amy hoped that the locals would be different from the lake people. Although she had only met a few lakers, they all appeared to be transient, inhabiting their exorbitant mansions in the summer months and returning to houses on Beacon Hill or rich suburban Boston for the rest of the year. Their expensive powerboats sped down the lake at dawn and dusk and were dusted off for only 3 months of the summer. They did not seem to follow any rules other than their own and policed the lake themselves.

She had always felt uneasy when meeting these lakers as they seemed to view her more as a curiosity than a potential friend or neighbor, but she chose not to dwell on that. They pulled up and parked at the local bar.

"We're here, let's go!" Amy and Patty joyfully voiced their enthusiasm and entered the bar and began to socialize.

The place was jam-packed. People were dancing, drinking, playing pool, darts and generally having a merry old time. As they entered the bar, Amy immediately scanned the rooms for friendly faces and spotted Shay.

"Hiya, Shay! You want to play doubles? We'll run the table!" She laughed ecstatically.

Shay beamed back at her. "Sure thing baby." He sauntered over and placed some coins on the pool table to book the next game.

She had met Shay once before when she brought in a co-worker to play 8 ball and had struck up a conversation with this handsome local pool shark. He was a champion pool player, but she had managed to beat him in a few games and looked forward to being his doubles partner.

"You, OK if I play some pool, Patty?" Amy asked hopefully of her cousin.

"No worries, kiddo, I'll just set myself up at the bar and I'll be fine." She lifted her small figure onto the high bar stool. Her voluminous breasts just peeked out of her shirt and she smiled flirtatiously at me.

"Girls are good to go." She grasped one in each hand lovingly. "Bring on those locals." She leaned over and whispered in her ear, "Where's that racoon guy now?"

Amy and Shay ran the pool table for hours as Patty engaged the local cowboys and everything was fine until a laker woman Amy knew approached her and smiled.

Her smile did not give away her warning. "You have to get out here now! Say nothing, just leave."

"What's going on?" Amy was confused.

The laker woman replied quietly, "They don't like you here. Leave quickly!" The sense of urgency in the laker woman's voice worried her.

"WTF!" she said under her breath and casually sauntered over to Patty.

"We have to go now, right now!" Her voice was quiet but authoritative.

Patty had a good buzz on and could not really comprehend the urgency of the exit.

Amy took a quick minute to size up the place. There were two exit doors she noticed as she scanned the run-down bar. Huge tall cowboys were monitoring them. *OMG, that guy looks just like the scary, crazy albino who used to whip himself, from the movie the Da Vinci Code,* she thought.

"Crap, Opus Dei is here. What the fuck!" she uttered a little too loudly on seeing the albino bouncer at the door.

A circle of women was surrounding Patty and grew more and more vocal, and high pitched. Patty was obviously not bonding with the local women as much as the men, which was not surprising. She quickly approached them to smooth things over but was stopped abruptly by an elbow in the stomach.

She bent over from the blow and hissed, "What the fuck! You bitch!" and quickly maneuvered her head away from another elbow.

"Time for you to go slut! Bye bye!" a voice said as she found herself flying across tables and chairs.

Patty screamed, "You fucking bitches leave my cousin alone!"

Amy was paralyzed for a minute trying to figure out what happened. As she stroked her hair, tufts of long curls came away in her fingers. She could see her cousin's fists flying widely into the crowd of women. It was a down and out free-for-all chick fight.

Her adrenalin got pumping and she moved towards the throng of women. "Let's do it, mother fuckers, you want this. Who's first?" she yelled, looking at the women encircling her. "I'm ready now, let's go!"

As they closed in, Amy took aim and swung at her closest assailant. It connected but both of her arms were promptly grabbed from behind, dragging her away. The power of the grasp was not female as she immediately realized.

"Shit, it's the Opus Deist!" Amy gasped breathlessly as she caught a glimpse of him.

A guy in a black cowboy outfit opened the exit door for the screaming woman and the Opus Dei doppelganger. She was thrown outside unceremoniously into the dust in front of the bar. The black costumed cowboy began to hurl insults at her as she lay on the ground, confused and bewildered.

"Who do you think you are coming in here tonight messing with our women folk? You're not from around these parts!" He walked menacingly around her.

Not giving her a chance to reply, he gave her an unmerciful kick with his cowboy boot into her abdomen. The voices surrounding her got louder and bolder. She was still reeling, catching her breath after hitting the ground and rolled up in a fetal position. Her assailant kicked her again.

Oh my God no. She briefly looked up from the ground and saw she was surrounded by more men now. They were yelling something about their women folk and began to take turns kicking her.

Blow after blow Amy took, arms shielding her head, until she realized she might die right there. These guys were not stopping. Her whole body was being kicked from top to bottom. She looked up and saw a skinny, small, blond male, who wasn't more than 20 years old grinning at her. It was his turn now!

"What are you doing? Why are you doing this? This isn't right! Stop! Stop! Stop right now! Please! Please!" she begged while looking into the crowd of men's eyes, gazing from one to the other, ensuring eye contact, gradually pulling herself to her feet.

Amy was surprised that they let her get up, but she knew it was a matter of survival. She caught a glimpse of the Opus Dei guy watching over the proceedings. It was not her cries of reasoning that stopped her assailants, he had called a halt to the beating.

She approached him cautiously and appealed to him crying, "OK, we'll go. We'll leave now. Let us go."

But then Amy realized that Patty was nowhere in sight. She was still in the bar when Amy was forcefully man-handled out.

"Where's my cousin? Is she still inside? Where is she?" Amy cried at the Opus Dei giant while she imagined finding Patty's beaten corpse inside the bar, a fate that she herself had just narrowly avoided. "Let me in. Let me in!" But, the albino Opus Deist ignored her pleadings and pushed her aside, barricading the door.

By now the women were joining the men who had assaulted her outside. The bar had emptied out into the parking lot. People were shouting at her, and she thought she heard some racial slurs, and tried her best to avoid close contact with any of the angry mob congregating outside.

Thank God I got up off the ground, she thought, *or else all these mother fuckers would be joining in,* as she tried to hide into the shadows.

"The police are coming. They should be here soon. They'll sort your fucking Puerto Rican ass out," a voice yelled out.

Thank God, she thought with relief. *These fuckers just tried to kill me. The cops will sort out this mess. These mother fuckers are going down for assault. All of them, especially that Opus Dei guy, that cowboy in black and that blond piece of shit excuse for a male. Patty and I will be saved from these fucking redneck shits.*

She had high hopes of being rescued as she gathered her wits and scanned the crowd outside for her cousin again, but she was nowhere in sight. Amy screamed her name and ran around the long one-story building and found her beside a dumpster, her shirt ripped from her torso, in shock. Patty also had an encounter with some cowboys at the back of the bar.

"Oh my god, are you OK?" she asked her. Muffled sobs and incomprehensible vocal sounds came from Patty's mouth.

They gathered themselves together, went to the car and locked the doors, hiding from the hostile mob around them and waited patiently for the police to rescue them. A single police officer in a cruiser arrived and Amy felt a sense of relief.

"It will be okay," she told her cousin, "the police are here. They will help us. They will arrest everyone!"

As the policeman got out of his car, he called to some of the women by name. Amy could see them gesticulating wildly and pointing at them in the car. As the policeman approached the car, they got out and started to explain the situation.

"We were attacked! Arrest them, all of them!" Amy pleaded with the officer to arrest their attackers, pointing at the men who stood nearby, who had repeatedly kicked her, and the ones who molested her cousin.

"You come with me, you're under arrest!" The police officer responded abruptly and forced her arms behind her back and pushed her over to his cruiser and threw her into the back of the car by her hair.

"What the fuck is going on? Not again!" she screamed from the inside of the locked police car, "You were supposed to rescue me, not arrest me!" Her frustration exploded, and she reacted like a wounded animal screaming, yelling and kicking. After damaging a foot trying to smash the window out, Amy realized that she wasn't going anywhere. Police cars were designed to be indestructible for a reason. But she had worked up some energy and heat inside the police vehicle, so she scrawled some obscenities on the fogged up rear window.

FUCK YOU REDNECK BASTARDS! She wrote carefully so the mob could read it clearly as they peered in at her, laughing. She sat resigned in the back of the police car until she heard another siren.

The police officer had called for another cruiser for Patty's transport to the station a few minutes away. At the station, they were handcuffed to a bench, ridiculed and derided by the police staff. Both were made to endure mug shots and fingerprinting. Patty was crying uncontrollably so they took her to the hospital for a full examination. The arresting officer marched Amy into a small cell and locked the door behind her. She sat on the cot dejectedly until she noticed a video camera and smiled. *If they wouldn't listen, I will get my story on videotape,* and began her speech to the camera.

"My civil rights have been violated. I have been arrested for no reason. I have been attacked and my attackers have been set free. They have jailed me instead of the people who assaulted me. The police officer assaulted me before he heard my story. He threw me into his cruiser by the hair on my head. I have not been read my Miranda rights! My civil rights have been violated on this night!"

She did not know if they were really recording but it gave her some satisfaction and she knew it bothered the police staff as they were yelling at her to shut up, so she continued for what seemed like an eternity.

The police gave her one phone call finally. She persuaded a good friend of hers, Mari, to bail them out. Mari arrived, and they waited together until Patty returned from the hospital. Patty just wanted to get out of there as soon as possible and Mari obliged readily. They were quiet in the car but when they got to Amy's lake house, they recounted the preceding chaos and assault to Mari.

After they both calmed down, Mari put the two cousins to bed and drove to her own house 30 minutes away. Mari was shocked, but that dive bar had a reputation for rednecks and racial bias anyway. *Not surprising really*, she mused as she tucked herself into bed for the night and sighed, *it's always drama with those two!*

As the next day dawned, the two cousins tended their wounds and relived the horrific night again. Amy suddenly saw a note in the door.

"It's a fucking citation for assault and battery against me!" screamed Amy. "Those mother fuckers kicked the shit out of me. I could have died, and I get a citation against me!" She was incredulous. "Is someone giving the guys who attacked us a citation?" She was hysterical. "Where are the guys who beat us up? I'm going up to the police station and sort this out!" She stormed out and left Patty behind in disbelief.

Patty was not OK after last night's events. She was glad Amy had not pressed her to go to the police station. She sat on the couch and sighed, *what a fucking nightmare!*

Amy drove aggressively to the police station. She was not going to be pushed out of her lake house by some redneck assholes. When she got to the police station, she demanded to press charges against her assailants. The police officer blankly refused to take her complaints.

"My boss arrested you and your friend last night, so I can't go up against him," the officer on duty stated. "He's my superior and that wouldn't look good now would it?"

She was aghast at his statement and stormed out of the police station screaming, "I'll be back! This local town bullshit, is going too far!"

Amy drove determinedly to the local Walmart and purchased an instamatic camera, and then returned to the lake house. She got Patty to take pictures of her bruised body which was covered in small polka dots from the pointy cowboy boots and the larger boot prints had also left their sickly marks.

"What you think, Patty? You want to sue these mother fuckers?"

She replied tiredly, "I don't know. I'm still reeling from everything."

Amy moved slowly but determinedly, her body sore and bruised. "Well I'm going to the doctor to get all this documented. You want to come with me?" She limped towards the door. Every painful step reminded her of the awful assault and her imprisonment in the police car.

"No thanks, I'm going to rest, but if you want to sue, I'm definitely up for that!" Patty said, regaining some of her spirit.

Amy arrived at the doctor's office and was ushered in immediately by a suspicious secretary. Dr. Mann was appalled at what had happened. He recommended a private detective to track down the people involved in her assault.

She began to get dressed. "That's a great idea, Dr. Mann."

"And I recommend hiring a good lawyer too, no public defender." Sympathy showed in his eyes.

"Will do, thanks for the advice." She slowly left, smiling briefly at the curious secretary on the way out.

So, a private detective and a fancy lawyer, crap this was going to cost, she mused, *but it'll be worth it to see those redneck assholes convicted of assault, especially the Black Bandit,* as Amy now called one of her assailants, *and the Opus Deist and the blond pathetic ass wipe,* who was yet to be nicknamed.

On returning to the lake house, she saw Patty sitting outside sunning herself and Shay was with her.

Amy greeted him angrily, "Shay, what happened last night? Where did you go? All hell broke loose after you left."

"Yeah, I heard they beat the shit out of some Puerto Ricans, so I wasn't really bothered about it. Now I hear it was you two guys? What happened?" Shay shifted his frame awkwardly in the lounge chair.

The cousins relayed the story to Shay who kept on shaking his head in disbelief.

"I can't believe it. I'm sorry I left. This wouldn't have happened if I was there." He left shortly after hearing their plight and was really no comfort for the 2 cousins.

"Did you see that? Once he heard about the charges against me, he ran out of here like a bat out of hell. And Puerto Ricans? We no more look like Puerto Ricans than the 2 Swedish chicks out of Abba. Although I did go to the same high school as JLo, does that count?" Amy laughed a little, but her heart wasn't in it.

Patty was slowing coming back to normal. "But you can't move or sing like her. Guess they didn't see our freckles eh? But they sure picked up on our Bronx accents! Bronx forever! Fuck those rednecks!" She jumped up and began to dance.

The next day was the hearing at the local courthouse. Patty's lawyer, although a public prosecutor, managed to get her charges of disorderly conduct dropped. Amy's case was sent the nearest biggest city, at her lawyer's request, to have a broader, unbiased jury pool for the disorderly conduct and assault charge pending against her. Patty had decided to leave from the courthouse but was reluctant to leave Amy alone.

"Be careful Amy, these locals are as crazy as the police force that supports them. Did you see that cop who arrested us at the court house? He was testifying about another case, 2 kids who flipped a car. The driver was OK, but the passenger got thrown out of the car. When the cop arrived on the scene, he gave the kid lying in the street a ticket for not wearing a seat belt. The kid got thrown out of the car and was being loaded into the ambulance and the cop gave him a freaking ticket! That's one crazy mean mother fucker!"

Amy looked tiredly at her cousin. "Yeah, the cops are a piece of work around here. Don't worry, by the time my case comes up, we'll have them by the short and curlies." She tried to smile and hoped that this would be true, hoped that the private eye would turn up something and hoped that the lawyer was going to be worth the money.

"Love ya," she said.

"Right back at ya!" The two women tenderly hugged each other and fell silent in the embrace.

Once Patty left, Amy tried to settle back and relax but found it difficult. The constant throbbing in her ankle and leg from the unyielding contact with the police cruiser window and door was a reminder of the night from hell. Her thoughts raced about the assault.

Hell, guess I'm just lucky to be alive. People have died from being kicked to death. And isn't being kicked with a shod foot, like a cowboy boot a felony? I'll slap those guys with felony lawsuits! See what the local cops think of that!

Over the next few weeks, she tried hard to fight the urge to sell off her lake home and return to the city, but that would mean that the rednecks won. And she was a fighter, so she persevered, hiring a private detective and a good defense lawyer, both of whom were Puerto Rican. Amy thought this slightly humorous. She imagined the detective, Eli, and the lawyer, Ricardo, questioning the rednecks about the attack. *Time for a different kind of racial pressure*, she thought. Eli had reported the locals were silent about the incident but that their eyes and body language screamed hatred and bigotry. She got some satisfaction from Eli's investigation of the rednecks, and she was hopeful that Ricardo would do his stuff in the courtroom, racial hatred and assault against two females. It seemed like a win, win to her.

As the months passed, Amy cruised the local streets, schools and shops, and saw many of her attackers. Although her soreness receded, her memory did not. She felt horror each time she saw one of the males and females who assaulted her, reliving her near-death experience.

She reduced her socialization with any townies. The local bar was off limits and she took solace in the fact that this was a private lake. The local riff raff was barred. Blue Lake and its inhabitants beckoned to her and she gladly accepted. Amy consoled herself, *I am safe on this lake. It's time to relax and enjoy my lakeside neighbors. Let the good times roll!*

Chapter 2

The New Neighbors

Finally, the eyesore of the neighborhood was razed, after years of having a steady stream of questionable tenants rent out the dilapidated, old, shit shack.

One middle aged, alcoholic, single guy finally drank himself to death, after that the Sheriff's Office came around for some young women. Also, one, seedy family with a terrifying German Shepherd attack dog, who menaced the neighborhood, came and left rather quickly.

The neighborhood was buzzing with speculation as to whom would move into the modern, gray house, a little incongruous-looking, more like a duplex apartment, but better than what was there!

They were a young couple, Steve and Vanessa Springer, with one little boy around two years old.

Samantha and David Blake, a couple in their forties, who have lived in the neighborhood for over ten years, lived across from them. They could see their house, but it was obscured by a small forest.

"Not the best place to live for such a young couple," David commented, as he and Samantha picked a few juicy, ripe tomatoes from their garden.

It was quite a diverse neighborhood, from millionaires to blue collar joes. Most families had lived there forever, passing down prized lakefront property from generation to generation. Most couples were at least in their fifties, with a few interesting characters thrown in, like Frank, the volatile, divorced Vietnam vet, suffering from PTSD. The typical 'get off my lawn' old crank who never missed an opportunity to make shit for his neighbors. But, more on him later.

"Mmm, true," Samantha agreed, plopping a sweet, cherry tomato into her mouth. "I would be happy with a wave and a hello." She smiled. "They probably just want to raise their family in a nice, rural area, with some privacy."

Indeed.

Time passed, and the new neighbors settled in. Apart from their dachshund coming into the Blake's yard to take a dump in their garden, it was pretty quiet.

One afternoon as David walked their English bulldog past their house, the dachshund came barreling out of the garage, yapping and jumping around Tank, the bulldog. He always enjoyed playing with other dogs, so David eased up on the leash and let the animals romp and sniff and run around.

Shortly after that, a tall, athletic blonde guy emerged from the garage door, limping slightly.

"Rocco!" he called to the dog, "get over here!" He flashed a sheepish smile at David. "Sorry."

"No worries." David laughed easily. "My dog doesn't get to play with other ones too often. I feel bad. It's good for neighborhood dogs to mingle and check each other out."

He chuckled. "True." He extended his hand. "I'm Steve."

"Welcome to the neighborhood." They shook hands. "David." He gestured towards his house. "I live over there."

"Nice."

They stood there awkwardly for a few minutes, as David scanned the yard, taking in all the fitness equipment, trying to think up a few pleasantries.

"You must be a fitness buff," he finally blurted out, feeling lame.

"I'm a personal trainer." He paused, a look of sadness and pain briefly flashed in his eyes. "I was an Olympics freestyle skier, even medaling a few times," he proudly stated, then grimaced. "Until I had a gnarly wipeout."

"Oh geez," David commiserated.

Steve sighed. "Yeah, I caught some major air and did an intense flip, but came down too hard and fast ... " He winced in remembrance, then continued, "Shattered my left leg, had to have major rods and pins put in, weeks of rehab." He frowned. "Career ending."

"Shit, how devastating."

"Totally." He shook his head. "But there's always a risk in daredevil sports."

"True."

"But, at least I'm still active, and I can still do quite a bit," he added. "I enjoy motivating people."

"Good for you, a positive attitude goes a long way." He called his dog, "Come on Tank, let's finish our walk." He turned to his new neighbor. "Hey, good to meet you. Thanks for letting my dog play around."

"No problem. We should do it again." He smiled cordially.

"Absolutely."

After that, Tank always excitedly led David over to their yard, looking for his new friend.

Once in a while, he would get lucky, having a good romp while David and Steve made small talk. Quite often, they would stroll by noticing the garage door half-closed, with just 2 sets of legs visible. Tank always tugged on his leash to go visit, but Dave held him back, not wanting to barge in on people.

One crisp fall day, as they were shooting the breeze in Steve's driveway again, a green pickup truck drove in. A thin, rather seedy-looking fellow emerged. He looked a little tense. They all nodded hello.

Steve glanced at him and quickly cut the conversation with Dave short. "Well we gotta go inside now," he stated, giving David the bum's rush.

"Yeah, of course. Let's go Tank!"

They departed. As he left the driveway, he turned to watch the men go into the garage and close the door halfway.

"Ah OK, I know what's going on here," he muttered to himself.

He returned home, unleashed the dog and grabbed a beer from the fridge. He plopped into his recliner by the fireplace and cracked open the brew.

"Aaah!" he exclaimed. "Nice." He smirked at his wife, sitting opposite him.

She knew that look. The 'I have a juicy tidbit' look. She let out an engaging laugh. "Alright," she said, playfully kicking his foot, "what do you have to tell me?" Her eyes sparkled.

He let out a chug of laughter. "You know me so well."

"Of course I do." She grinned.

"I think Mr. Olympic over there is dealing." He sipped his beer.

"What? Come on," she replied in a skeptical tone.

He put his hand up. "We were just chatting over there when some pale, weird dude dropped in and I was hastily given the heave-ho."

She crinkled her eyes. "That's it? Why would they want you to stay? That's pretty normal behavior." She shook her head.

He rubbed the stubble on his chin. "True, but there was a bizarre vibe in the air — and they promptly went into the garage and shut it most of the way."

She shrugged her shoulders. "Pretty flimsy evidence."

He ruminated for a moment, then spoke again, "It's not the first time I've seen legs standing in the garage." He continued as she laughed, "Come to think of it, I've seen cars come and go from there all times of the day, sometimes fiddling in the mailbox."

"Really?"

"Yes."

Samantha sighed and stroked her hair. "Well, that would be too bad. A young couple like that with a cute little boy." She looked at her husband. "Have you met the wife?"

"No."

"Me neither."

He raised his eyebrows. "Another thing. I haven't seen people coming to their house to use all that workout equipment, either. Have you?"

Her eyes widened. "Holy shit, you're right." She paused. "How could we have not noticed that?"

"I guess we're not that nosey." Dave chuckled charmingly.

She smiled. "Personal trainer, my ass."

One day, when Samantha was collecting her mail, she found a piece that belonged to the new couple.

"Now I have an excuse to go over and see what's going on," she said aloud to herself.

No one was outside, there was a car in the yard. She walked up the pathway and knocked on the door. After a while, a young, blonde opened the door. She could be very pretty, but on this day her long, blonde hair was kind of a rat's nest, looked to be in need of a good wash. She had deep bags under her eyes and was quite ashen. She stood in the doorway.

Samantha tried to hide her shock at the woman's appearance. "Hi ... um, I'm your neighbor and a piece of your mail accidentally ended up in my mailbox," she stammered quickly, forcing a smile.

The woman continued to stand in the doorway. "Oh, OK, thanks." She grabbed the envelope and abruptly shut the door.

Samantha turned to go home. She let out a long breath. *OK then, I guess I won't be invited in for a cup of tea*, she thought sarcastically, kind of disappointed and a trifle offended. She enjoyed being at least cordial to her neighbors and vice a versa.

Later, she relayed her interaction with the woman to Dave as they sat down to dinner.

"So, I met the lady over there," she informed him as she stabbed a cucumber from her salad and began chewing.

"Really? Finally." He nodded his head. "How'd it go?"

She let out a short laugh. "Pretty uneventful," she said sardonically.

He chuckled.

"We got their mail, so I delivered it." She took another bite of salad, then went on, "Some haggard-looking young broad came to the door, grabbed her mail and pretty much closed the door." She shrugged her shoulders. "A bit rude really, no introduction, but whatever."

Dave was eagerly diving into his steak. "Haggard? Hmm…interesting." He flashed a grin at his wife. "Now do you believe me?" he teased good-naturedly.

She finished swallowing, then responded. "Yeah, unfortunately." She shook her head. "A damn shame." She leveled a serious look at Dave. "Let's just stay out of it. I don't want to get embroiled in neighborhood drama."

He nodded. "Yep, I agree."

Summer turned to fall, which was beautiful on the lake, the crisp air, things quieting down, but all too soon winter barges in.

During the winter, the neighborhood becomes a bit of a ghost town, the summer people have closed up shop, older ones go to Florida. No more sitting out on the deck, with the tantalizing smell of your neighbor's barbecue wafting deliciously in the air. No more laughter and pieces of conversation floating around as the boats cruise by.

People basically hibernate in the cold months, as it gets quite snowy and bitter in the area. You rarely see your neighbors, just hear the hum of snow blowers and the scraping of snow shovels.

There were no sightings of the reclusive pair, and Dave and Samantha both noted various automobiles coming and going.

In early March, as Samantha walked the dog around the block, she just happened to catch the two emerging from their vehicle and heading into the house. It was her first glimpse of the guy, and she was taken aback.

He was quite gaunt-looking, disheveled, wan, and very sickly-looking as if he had AIDS or cancer.

What the hell? That's the frailest, least-robust looking personal trainer I've ever seen, she thought sadly, as she watched them enter the house and hung back, staying away. She also noticed the wife, still looking like death warmed over, was pregnant, possibly three months. *Tragic*, she thought.

Back at her place, she sat down by the cozy stove as Dave stoked the fire.

"Saw the neighbors, he looks like absolute hell too." She frowned.

"Oh yeah?" he asked, surprised. "He looked fine when I saw him." He put one more log on the fire, then sat down. "Winter must be hard for him, for personal training," he said in a sarcastic tone.

"Indeed." She pursed her lips. "So, they're both junkies."

A disgusted look crossed his face. "That's usually how it ends up."

She held up a finger. "Oh yeah, it gets worse ... she's pregnant."

"Sonofabitch." He wearily ran a hand through his hair. "I don't know what to say or do…" He sighed.

"We could call DSS."

He threw her a sharp look. "Get that poor little boy yanked out of there?" He shook his head. "We already agreed to stay out of it. I don't want to cause a shitstorm." He grimaced, and continued, "If she's pregnant, then the doctor or a nurse or whoever will be smart enough to help her out," he reasoned. "Let them do their job."

"True," she agreed.

Several weeks later, Dave ran into the UPS man, Harry, who always stopped and gave the dog a bone, so they were quite friendly at this point. Harry of course, being a delivery man on the same route for years, was quite familiar with most of the area. He loved to gossip and always had some tantalizing story to tell. He had a particularly juicy little nugget today.

"You know that personal trainer over there?"

"Yes, we talk from time to time," Dave replied warily, "seems decent." *Remember to stay out of it, don't add your speculation,* he told himself.

Harry laughed. "Yeah, well, he was just arrested for a bunch of shit," he supplied easily, a gleam in his eye.

Dave's head went back. "No, really? Damn."

"Possession of heroin, coke, and some other vehicle violations."

"Wow." He feigned surprise. "You never know what's going on behind closed doors do you, even in the boonies." He clapped Harry on the shoulder. "Or maybe you do," he teased.

Harry smiled broadly. "I've seen some shit. Most of the time you don't want to know ... "

Dave rubbed his scruff thoughtfully. "I can believe that."

After that, Samantha and Dave tried to steer clear of the troubled duo. They did notice garbage piling up on the back staircase and cars continued to frequent the property.

"What the hell is going on over there?" David mused to Samantha. "I guess he didn't go to jail. His clients keep rolling in." He agitatedly rubbed the back of his neck.

She exhaled an exasperated breath. "I'm surprised some neighbor hasn't called the Board of Health — especially the rich, snobby ones."

"I know." He rolled his eyes. "We still keeping our noses out of it?"

She came to him and put her arms around his waist. "Yes." She looked deeply into his warm brown eyes. "We don't need to get gunned down by some strung-out druggie."

He cringed. "Right." He hugged her tightly and gave her a loving kiss.

He didn't know it then, but soon he would be right in the thick of it.

One afternoon in mid-August, while walking Tank through the trails in the woods that abut the neighborhood, Dave noticed something at the base of a big oak tree. Gingerly moving forward, he could see a pair of legs jutting out. Not wanting to interrupt a couple engaging in a little afternoon delight, he turned away quietly.

But something made him pause. He didn't see a second pair of legs — or hear any noise. He headed back to investigate, a sick feeling swept over him.

He approached the tree and cranked his head around. There was Steve, slumped over, unconscious, with a syringe stuck in his arm.

"Jesus! No! Steve!" He shook him, slapped his face slightly. No response. He whipped out his phone and called 911.

"Yes, hi, I found an unresponsive male in the woods off of Grandchester Lane, needle in arm."

He brought his hands to his face. "Shit, what do I do? Steve!" he yelled. "Wake up! Think of your kids!"

He didn't want to leave him but wanted to get Steve's wife here. He called his wife.

"Hello?"

"Samantha! Get over to the new neighbor's house — get the wife — Steve's overdosed in the woods!"

"What?" Her voice was shrill. "OK! OK!"

She raced to the house and banged on the door. "Vanessa! Open the door! It's an emergency!"

No response.

"Please come to the door!" she pleaded.

"Hell with this!" She tried the door. It was open. She raced around the house screaming for her. She only found the little boy — playing on the floor of his room with his toy train.

"This just gets better and better." She sighed and phoned Dave.

"What's going on?" he asked, highly agitated.

"She's not here — the boy is here alone."

"What! Oh, for Christ sake!"

"I can't leave him alone — or take him out there."

"No, no, of course not."

"How is —"

"Gotta go, the medics are here." He ended the conversation.

"Do you know this man?" one asked while preparing to administer the Narcan shot.

"Just in passing — he's my neighbor. But everyone pretty much keeps to themselves." He wasn't going to get ensnared in this mess.

"I see." He examined Steve's arm. "Lots of tracks — pretty hardcore user."

Dave put a hand over his mouth and shook his head.

The EMT looked at him suspiciously. "What are you doing out here?"

Great, here we go, he thought, irritated. *I had to find him.* "I was walking my dog," he replied, as he watched them tend to Steve. "I'm not into this fucking shit!" he shouted, now fuming. "You wanna see my arms?" He held them out. "I don't have any goddamned tracks! I had to be the poor sap to find him!"

"All right — calm down!"

"I don't need this shit!"

The shot was given and miraculously he came around.

"Phew! Thank God!" Dave stood back to let them check his vitals. "Steve? Are you OK?"

He was groggy and listless and looked around, dazed. "Where am I?"

"In the woods." Dave couldn't mask the look of disgust on his face. "Where is your wife? My wife found your boy alone in the house."

"What? Oh shit." He rested his head against the tree and tried to gather his bearings. He looked like a corpse. "Um…She's in the hospital ... she gave birth a month early," he told him, his voice soft and pained.

Dave could put two and two together. The baby was hooked on opioids. He felt sick to his stomach. He wanted to punch this guy in the face.

He clenched his fist. "So, what the hell are you doing out here?" he raged at him. "Killing yourself? That will help everyone out, you jackass!" He stabbed a finger at him. "You have two innocent little kids now!"

Steve remained quiet, still pathetically propped up against the tree.

"You and your wife better get your shit together," he ground out. "Good luck keeping your children now ... you should lose them!"

Just then, a policeman was approaching the scene and overheard Dave's tirade and horned in. "We are taking your child into Protective Services — and you're under arrest. Get up! If you can get your sorry ass up."

Steve rose unsteadily and started to protest. "You can't take my kid. Please don't do this," he pleaded in a shaky voice.

The policeman laughed harshly. "We can take him, and we are. We know you have priors, tough shit."

He grabbed him and cuffed him and began leading him out of the woods. He began flipping out, struggling and screaming and kicking the cop.

"Go ahead asshole, let's add assault on a police officer!"

"Fuck you, man!"

"I'll taze your ass!"

Dave followed them out silently, shaking his head at the whole sorry scene.

As they came past Steve's house, Dave saw his wife peeking out the door, keeping the boy safely in the house. She also was shaking her head and almost in tears.

He joined his wife and gave her a warm hug. "How awful!"

They stood together and watched the cop place Steve in the back of the cruiser.

The policeman then came over to them. "Um ... sorry to involve you folks, but could you stay with the boy until the social worker gets here — she shouldn't be too long."

"Yeah, sure, of course," Samantha replied wearily.

"Thanks." He then walked away.

As they watched the ambulance and cruiser pull away, Dave commented wryly, "Aren't you glad we were able to stay out of this?"

She let out a sarcastic laugh and smiled at him. "Oh yeah."

All was quiet at that house for a good month, and Samantha and Dave were grateful for the drama-free neighborhood.

Then, Vanessa returned home with her new baby, and after a while Steve returned.

"I guess everything turned out well for them," he commented to his wife as they raked leaves.

She glanced over into the neighbor's yard. "Oh, I'm glad." She smiled warmly. "One big scare was enough to set them straight, I hope."

They, once again stayed out of it, even walked their dog in the other direction if anyone was around.

One day, as Dave was washing his truck in the driveway, he noticed a coroner's van backing into their yard. A sense of dread dropped into his stomach.

"Christ, no." He started to shake, and felt bile rise in his throat.

He wanted to turn away, but as human nature goes, he couldn't. He watched them carry a body bag out, followed by Vanessa. Her bloodcurdling screams rent the air. Dave covered his mouth and kept down the urge to vomit. He had to go in his house.

He walked in like a zombie, his face devoid of color.

Samantha almost dropped the dish she was putting away as she noticed her husband's ghostly complexion. "My God, what is it?" She rushed to him.

He crushed her against him and stroked her hair. "Something terrible has happened over there ... " he choked out and nodded in the direction of the tragic house.

She inhaled sharply. "No!" She wailed, her eyes wide and glistening.

He stroked her cheek. "I think Steve is gone."

"No!" She shrieked this time.

Chapter 3

Camp Booby Trap

It was the summer weekend retreat house for Sharon and Pete Sampson. Pete was an electrical engineer, handsome, tall and a former college athlete. He took pride in his appearance and ate healthy, organic fruits and vegetables, non-GMO only, high in fiber and protein, and took his colonic health and vitamin pills daily. He did Birkham yoga daily to compensate for his alcoholic tendencies which was slightly revealed in his three-month pregnant like paunch. Nonetheless, his general appearance was one of fitness and health, and he tried to maintain his Adonis like physique. His job gave him some satisfaction, but he shied away from moving up the ladder in the company as it would mean no more weekends on Blue Lake. His company's headquarters was overseas and a promotion would require a move and he was not amenable to that.

His wife, Sharon, was also intensely beautiful. Her cream colored, flawless skin matched her hazel eyes. Secretly, she met with the cosmetologist monthly and received beauty enhancing Botox injections and other skin rejuvenation therapies to maintain her wrinkle free existence. She was comparable to many models on the cover pages of Cosmopolitan or Vogue, although time was beginning to show some handicap of her age. Her figure was like Marilyn Monroe but not the size 14, more like a size 10.

She had met Pete at a friend's party and they have fallen head over heels in love. They made a spectacular couple. She had been an aspiring actress but most of her roles ended up being at the local mall as an elf at Santa's workshop, so she gave up. After their marriage, she no longer diligently pursued an acting career, although she did a little community theater. She settled into the role of domesticity easily. She loved yoga and dreamed about becoming a yoga instructor. She had heard about yoga with goats and was considering checking out a class for amusement. Her friend, Kari, had mentioned one in Boston that they should go to.

Pete had inherited the cottage on the lake from his grandparents. He was the only grandchild. His parents lived in St. Thomas so they had no interest in the chilly lake side retreat in New England.

Every weekend in the summer for the past 15 years, Pete and Sharon went to the lake. Their family had never expanded with children. But that suited them both as they never felt the biological need to have a child tugging at their clothes. Their life was active without them, socializing with friends in Boston and they had managed to make some friends on the lake too, so life was not boring or unfulfilled.

The lake house was small by some standards, one bedroom, bathroom, living room, fireplace, and a dining room with 2 glass double sliders inviting one to appreciate the lake view. But after 15 years of weekends, Sharon felt an uneasy feeling of disinterest. She didn't know quite how to figure it out, but something was definitely up. The house seemed to be smothering her recently. She used to find Pete's fetish collecting anything with boobs, or breasts, amusing. But now she was having nightmares in which a big breasted female was suffocating her with an overly zealous hug.

Over the years, Pete's collection had expanded to the point of no return. Every available nook, cranny, table and shelf held some sort of knickknacks with boobs, or references to boobs. There was lobsters, dogs, cats, roosters and moose adorned with breasts. Salt and pepper shakers, tea pots, sunglasses, hats, cups and glasses all came with breasts or nipples. Posters, magazines and books scattered around the house, extolled the beauty of the female breasts.

OMG the house should have been named Booby Trap because it certainly felt like that, Sharon mused to herself.

She was trapped and needed some time away from this breast laden abode. *Maybe Pete's mom never breast fed him.* She smiled. She had never asked him but pondered on this now.

"What you thinking about? You're looking a bit dazed?" Pete said as he sauntered by her.

"Just dreaming about you honey," she replied.

"Dreaming about getting a boob job?" he asked. "You should think about it honey, you look great, but things could be even greater!"

She smiled unevenly at him. This was not the first time he had mentioned breast enlargements.

"Yes, honey I am definitely up for that!" Sharon turned her back to him. "I have an appointment made at the clinic," she lied. *At least it was near cocktail hour and their boat cruise.* "Do you have the margaritas made?" She would need to do a few shots before their boat ride.

"Yes, I do. Just the way you like them. And don't forget to bring the straws." Pete chuckled at her.

"I'll be right along, just have to tinkle first and I'll meet you down at the dock. Get the boat running." She watched him leave the house with a cooler of margaritas and glasses. "Don't forget the straws" she mimicked him, "the ones with the boobs ha, ha, ha, ha, ha, what the fuck? Lord let me get out of here." She prayed as she gulped down her second shot of tequila.

"Are you ready darling?" Pete's voice carried up to her from the lake. She didn't have to hear him really, as their life had become predictable.

"Coming!" She gave him the thumbs up sign as she realized he couldn't hear her over the boat's motor running.

Sharon clad in her 2-piece bikini, with numerous accessories, sunglasses, cover-up and scarf and headed down to the lake with appetizers and boob straws in hand.

"Let's get moving," Pete enthusiastically said.

There were going to pick up Scott and Emma Daniel, a couple with whom they made friends. They too, were young and vivacious. Scott Daniel and his wife Emma were real estate brokers and spent the winter in Boston. In the summer, they moved to the lake and commuted to Boston daily. The commute was worth it, they had explained to Pete and Sharon.

Sharon called Emma on her cell phone, "Hey come on, it's 4 o'clock! Margaritas are on board calling your names!"

"We're ready, be right there," Emma answered, "come on Scott." The phone clicked dead.

Not a minute later, the boat docked at the Daniel's house.

"Hey Pete, how's it going?" Scott greeted them from the shore.

"What! No hello for me?" Sharon stood up and smiled. "Thanks for asking Scott."

"He has no manners, don't mind him!" Emma climbed on board. "How are you my darling Sharon?"

"Okay, but will be better after this margarita for sure!" Sharon gulped her drink down unceremoniously.

"Great, margaritas for everyone then!" Emma smiled over at Pete and poured drinks for everyone.

"Cast off mate!" Pete indicated at the rope for Scott to untie it from the dock.

"Ay yi, Captain Birdseye. We're ready to party!" Scott untied the boat and deftly got onboard for their afternoon cruise.

After a round of drinks, the 2 couples cast the anchor in the center of the lake. The women were sunbathing while the men prepared more drinks.

"Ready for some poker ladies?" Scott said, ogling Sharon's breasts.

"Sure thing!" responded Emma who really enjoyed seeing Pete's tanned body glistening with sweat in the sun. Emma herself was always game for a little nudity but she got the impression that Sharon wasn't quite feeling the same about their little strip poker game. *Scott wasn't a prize, but he wasn't that bad,* Emma thought. It had always been fun on previous trips, but she sensed something amiss.

"Hey, are you okay?" Emma looked over at Sharon who was staring out into space.

"Sure thing! Let's get the game started." The tequila drove Sharon's enthusiasm forward.

Pete brought out the card table and the game began. After a few hands, Emma was topless, but Sharon was still in her bikini, thanks to her coverslip, sunglasses and hat. Pete was the first one to be totally naked.

"Birthday suit number 1, here's coming at you," Pete said, "you're next." He poked at Emma with his finger.

"Just you wait!" Emma laughed at Pete's prodding finger and felt a throbbing between her legs.

"Hey I'm hot," said Sharon. "How about a dip?" She loved swimming in the lake. It was so clean and refreshing. "Join me?" She got up and dove abruptly into the water.

"Sure!" said Pete. His naked body followed her quickly into the water.

"Me too!" Scott dove after them.

"Wait for me!" Emma dove carelessly into the clear blue water.

Thanks goodness, Sharon thought, *Emma's drooling over Pete is a pain in my ass. She's gotta tighten up! Or I'll say something I'll regret if she doesn't!* She was beginning to feel the tequila rushing though her body and swam hastily towards the boat.

"I'm done," she yelled back at her naked husband.

The three others remained swimming for some time while Sharon toweled off. She picked up her binoculars and amused herself by bird watching. She did enjoy these little boating excursions. Although the strip poker with the two males and Emma left her emotionless. They had nothing that she wanted to see. She surveyed the shoreline looking at the shacks and mansions that dotted the landscape. There was a heavily forested shore further up where bald eagles nested, and she scoured the tree line for signs of life. The three other boaters climbed aboard.

"Shall we finish our game?" Pete asked.

Sharon turned to Emma and smirked.

"Another day perhaps? Let's motor on." The look on Sharon's face was enough for Emma to call it quits. "I've seen enough for today." She poked Pete in the ribs merrily.

Scott was disappointed that Sharon had accessorized so much that she was still fully clothed after their poker game, but now she was being a real bitch. "Fine by me, let's motor on," he agreed.

They continued around the lake gossiping and drinking. There was always something happening it seemed.

"Her daughter had her baby," Emma stated, pointing at the small yellow house. "Some Grandma she'll make!" She laughed.

"Their kid just got arrested for burglary," Scott said pointing at another. "Little apples don't fall far from the tree."

"There's the nudist camp," Pete said enviously wishing he was a member of that group.

They all gossiped freely about their neighbors feeling superior in some sort of way.

As they approached the forest lined shoreline, Sharon demanded, "Quiet! I want to see if the eagles are around." In the stillness, the 4 boaters gazed up to the trees. "It's nothing." Her voice echoed disappointment.

"Where are you looking?" Pete looked at his wife and then squinted up toward the wooded area.

"What's that at the base of the tree?" Emma gasped. "Oh my God Scott, it's a body! Maybe they're asleep or drunk?"

Sharon aimed the binoculars towards the shore line.

"Get moving Pete, over there!" Scott pointed toward the area.

Sharon admired his attitude of leadership.

"Maybe it's just a bunch of clothes? Last week, when I was out walking the dog, I found a bunch of clothes in the woods. I didn't tell anyone because I figured it was from the nudist camp. Maybe it's another nudist gone wild?" Emma was talking much too fast as she tried to calm her hysteria.

Before they got close to the shore, Sharon spied a case of beer on the shoreline. "It's OK! They are just drunk and sleeping. There's a case of beer and a Vodka bottle on the shore. Looks like whoever it is, is having a little rest. Leave them alone and let's go on."

"Sure thing honey." Pete steered the boat away from the shore and they continued around the lake soaking up the rays and more appetizers and tequila.

A shout from the shore called out, "Hey! You guys! What's going on?"

It was Mick. He was sitting in his lounge chair and beside him was Lorraine. She joined Mick in welcoming them.

"Come on in and park that boat. Join us for a cocktail?" Mick asked.

Their house had the most spectacular sunset views. From their dock one could watch the sun setting slowly into the cove, totally unobscured by trees. Every evening, they could be spied on their dock in their luxurious lounge chairs sipping and sun worshiping. Mick and Lorraine were a fun-loving couple. He was a hedge fund manager and she ran a local nonprofit organization.

"Sure thing," said Pete.

"We'd love to," chimed in Emma.

"Come on my beauty!" Scott encouraged Sharon to move off the boat onto the shore.

Sharon was a little unsteady on her feet and Emma helped her cautiously. Pete and Scott promptly tied up the boat and joined in the sun worshiping party. As the sun went down, the party of six sun worshipers sang songs.

"What about here comes the sun, do do do do, here comes the sun, do do do do and I said I'm alright do do do do do ... " Mick merrily sang out.

Lorraine bellowed out Elton John's, 'Don't Let The Sun Go Down On Me.'

Pete serenaded them with, "There is a house in New Orleans they call the rising sun ... "

"I got one," Sharon joined in. "Good day sunshine, good day sunshine, good day sunshine, I need to laugh when the sun is out. I got something I can laugh about. I feel good in a special way. I'm in love and it's a sunny day!"

They all joined in the chorus laughing and singing until the sun set for the evening.

After sunset, the lakeside grew colder.

"How about a bonfire? I just love a roaring fire at night!" Mick looked at the two other men enquiringly.

"Sure," said Pete, "we'll help get the wood for the fire." The three men set about placing wood into the fire pit, carefully arranging the smaller pieces at the bottom and increasing the size of the wood towards the top.

Mick and Lorraine's lakeside retreat had a marvelous stone patio set up. The hedge fund manager liked his high-tech toys and his taste expanded to outside living areas. Appliances like a built-in refrigerator, bar, sound system, and range surrounded a huge central fire pit which was as deep as it was wide.

"This is going to be a good one," said Mick, "many a pig has been roasted in this fire pit. Let's make it huge."

"Yes," Scott agreed.

Pete had other things on his mind though. "Hey, you guys ever hear anything about swingers on the lake?"

"Swingers!" Mick exclaimed, "You got to be frigging kidding me."

"Nothing that I ever heard about, just gossip." Scott added some more wood to the growing fire.

"Hey how's our Boy Scouts doing? You get that fire lit yet? Come on!" Lorraine pleasantly prodded them.

"Sure thing baby. We just got it going now," replied Mick.

Pete decided to leave the topic of swinging to another time as they joined the three females who now lounged in chairs around the fire pit. The singing started again.

"What about songs that have fire in them?" Emma suggested.

"I got one," said Sharon, "come on baby light my fire!"

"What about Jerry Lee Lewis? You shake my nerves and you rattle my brain. Too much love, drive a man insane. You broke my will, but what a thrill. Goodness gracious, great ball of fire!" Pete sang to Sharon who seemed in better form now and was smiling up at him.

He dragged her up into his arms and started to dance with her until she begged off to use the toilet.

"Hold on and I'll play it on all the speakers outside," said Mick.

As the music begin to play, the dancing picked up momentum.

"Hey this is what you meant by swinging Pete?" Mick demonstrated by twirling Lorraine under his arm and then over his back.

"Yeah!" enthused Lorraine, thoroughly enjoying the dancing activities.

Emma was sitting on the side taking a break when Pete grabbed her hand and pulled her up to dance.

"No this is what I meant!" He twirled Emma three times in one direction and three times in another. "Now we're swinging!" He released her laughing uncontrollably, his hands resting on his knees, and his body doubled over.

Sharon was in the house, refreshing her make up after visiting the ladies' room when she heard a piercing scream. *What was that? Was it hysterical laughing? Surely it was*, she thought to herself. *It was certainly not an eagle.* The screams got louder and louder. It was a woman's voice piercing into her brain. She ran outside to a hysterical scene. Lorraine was mute and seemed to be paralyzed at the side of the fire pit. The screams were coming from the fire pit! It was Emma! She had obviously stumbled into the roaring fire pit. The three men were scrambling and shouting at the same time.

"Emma! Emma!" Sharon sobbed.

"Oh my God, oh my God!"

"Get her out! Get her out!"

"Oh Christ, oh Christ!"

"Call 911, Sharon, call 911!"

Mick cautiously lowered himself closer to Emma in the pit. Pete and Scott gingerly helped him to lift Emma out. Her body was badly charred.

Sharon dialed 911. "Somebody's been burned in a fire. She's badly burned! We need an ambulance!" She relayed the information and address to the police dispatcher.

The dispatcher told Sharon to remove any burnt clothing and cover her with a clean cloth or sheet. Emma's dress had disintegrated in the fire. She was totally naked with a thin veil of smoke emanating from patches of her charred black and grey skin.

"Get a clean sheet!" demanded Sharon of Mick who raced to the house and promptly returned with it.

They covered Emma with it as she moaned and whimpered like a puppy.

After what seemed like ages, the faint ambulance siren got louder and louder until it finally reached them. The paramedics moved briskly in the cool night air, carefully putting Emma onto a stretcher. Pete and Mick helped them to carry her to the ambulance.

"It's OK, it's OK!" Scott whispered to Emma.

Emma appeared to be going into shock as Scott hopped into the ambulance and it raced off to the hospital. Pete and Mick returned to their wives at the fire pit.

"I'm done," said Mick awkwardly.

"I hope she's okay," said Lorraine.

"Let's hope and pray," agreed Sharon.

The two couples nodded their goodbyes in shocked silence. Pete and Sharon climbed onto their party boat and proceeded slowly back to their boob infested cottage.

In what seemed like hours later, Scott sent a text to everyone that Emma was okay, she was going to make it. She would need some skin grafts, but she would make it. What had been an evening full of drunkenness, mighty singing and fearless dancing had turned into a swinging nightmare.

"It's all my fault! It's all my fault!" Pete ashamedly admitted.

"It's OK, it's OK. She's going to be fine. She's going to be fine." Sharon stroked her husband's blonde hair, comforting him and drawing his head towards her bosom to rest on. After a few minutes passed she whispered, "Come on, let's go to bed now." She led him like a child, by the hand, through the multi-boobed cottage to their boob infested bedroom and sighed.

Chapter 4

It's Swing Time

On the other side of the lake, in a lovely A-frame with a big deck, lived a middle-aged couple, forty-somethings Sarah and Brian Cornell. They were high-school sweethearts, married rather young — no children. The phrase 'opposites attract' was invented for these two!

Sarah, relatively attractive, mousy brown hair, tall, thin — smart as a whip, college graduate and now a scientist working with stem cells.

Brian, quite portly, a shaved head due to male pattern baldness, high school dropout, working a variety of dead-end jobs, currently a forklift operator in a warehouse.

One must speculate if the poor woman had serious self-esteem issues to end up with him, but as they say love is love! They've been married 21 years.

As it goes with so many couples, especially childless, things have gotten stale as hell and their sex life has pretty much ground to a halt. Can you say middle age crisis!

As the couple sat on the deck, sipping red wine and watching a mallard duck family glide by on the lake, Sarah looked wistful.

She took a sip of her drink and sighed. "Do you ever regret not having children?"

Brian glanced over at his wife. "No, not really," he truthfully admitted. "You've always been a passionate career woman — and I really don't have a paternal bone in my body ... I enjoy the freedom to do what we want."

She laughed tightly. "That's true." She knit her brows together. "But ... there has to be something more than this ... " She gestured at the lake. "Sitting here like two oldsters whiling away the time." She pursed her lips.

Here we go, Brian thought to himself. He rolled his eyes. "And what do you suggest we do? Go on a cruise? Rent a motorhome and go cross country?" He looked pensive. "That would be memorable. We should do something like that at least once."

"Um ... perhaps someday, yes." She hesitated and nervously ran her hand through her hair.

He gave her a sharp look. "What the hell is going on?"

"Nothing, nothing," she reassured him, grasping his hand tightly.

Awkward silence hung briefly in the air.

"What do you want to tell me?" His blue eyes searched her face.

She anxiously blew out her breath as her eyes shifted to the calm, blue water. "I'd like to try swinging," she quickly replied.

Brian, quite frankly, looked taken aback ... and rather horrified. Then his visage darkened as he tightened his grip on her hand. "You're having a goddamned affair, aren't you?" he spat out. "I knew it. You women can never be content." His eyes became icy slits. "Or you just got tired of fatty over here with the menial job. When did you become so superficial?" He flung her hand away.

She tried to caress his cheek, he angrily turned away. "No, I'm not having an affair." She got up and stood against the deck railing. "I ... I just thought you might like a little excitement, variety." She turned towards him. "Seeing that I am the only woman you slept with — as far as I know," she said apprehensively.

He exploded out of the lounge chair and came to the railing. "You are the only woman I've ever had sex with, yes," he blurted out, looking stricken. "Do you know why?"

She remained silent.

"Look at me – I'm no Adonis, never have been," he stated. His voice was pained. "Always been the chubby kid, picked on, shunned, mercilessly harassed ... not the sharpest knife in the drawer ... and I've learned to live with that." He broke off and turned toward her, a loving look in his eyes. "And by some miracle I found you. I couldn't believe it."

Sarah smiled tenderly. "I have always accepted you for you, you know that." She paused. "I just thought that this might be good for both of us...enhance our sex life."

He nervously tapped the wood railing. "Maybe it would be — I think you're overlooking a huge deterrent here." He smiled thinly. "Me!"

She started to protest.

Brian held up his hand. "I'm flattered, babe, that you think anyone would actually want to screw me — but they won't." He grabbed his paunchy belly and ran a hand over his hairless pate. "I don't like to see myself naked, and you want to add insult to injury, make me feel even more like shit by having me be rejected by other women?" He was getting a little angry again. "No."

Sarah chuckled and rubbed his back. "Relax. I already have a couple lined up." She looked very mischievous.

His head went back. "What?"

"Yeah, you know that nice young couple we met when we went on the party boat hitch-up barbecue? When four party boats were tied together and we all cruised the lake for hours and partied?"

He looked up to the sky, ruminating. "Oh yeah. Melissa and Travis — thirties, very personable, seems like a load of laughs."

"And a load of sex." She grinned saucily.

"Excuse me?" His eyes lit up. "You mean to tell me you were out there talking about hooking up?" He shook his head playfully. "In mixed company? For God's sake, Sarah. You want us to get the reputation of being the lake perverts?" he grunted. "How about a little discretion? All this behind my back?"

She waved at him dismissively. "It wasn't out there, it was at the ladies of the lake book club. We were reading a particularly erotic book, so some of us got into a bit of playful ... conversation." She smiled wickedly. "On the down low, she approached me afterwards and wondered if I, we would be up for some fun."

He raised his eyebrows. "What a bold girl."

"Indeed." She playfully patted his bottom. "You'll have a lot of fun." Her eyes flashed as she giggled.

He put up his hands and laughed. "She's probably too much for me!"

So, the rendezvous was discreetly set up. Sarah invited the couple over for a lovely dinner.

The adventurous duo was Melissa and Travis Green. She is a bank teller and he a plumber.

They all relaxed in the living room with a nice bottle of Cabernet Sauvignon after their meal.

"Everything was delicious, thank you," Melissa stated, trying to make small talk.

"Yes, my compliments to the chef," Travis inserted a little awkwardly, hoisting his wine flute.

Nervous tension hung in the air like a light fog.

"So ... are you enjoying the lake?" Brian inquired.

"Yes, very much," Travis returned. "We take our kayaks out all the time, go into the cove, enjoy seeing the blue herons and sometimes turtles."

"There are lots of kayaks on this lake," Sarah chimed in.

"Yes — and party boats have really taken over," replied Melissa.

"Speaking of birds — have you seen the bald eagles?" Brian asked.

Their guests both shook their heads.

"Yeah, beautiful to see them diving over the lake. I think they live in the stand of pines behind the island."

"We will have to keep an eye out."

More silence as they looked around at each other, polite smiles plastered on their faces.

Finally, Brian spoke up, "Hell, I don't think this wine is going to cut it. How about something stronger?"

"Yes!" they all said in unison as Brian chuckled.

"Vodka? Tequila? Jack Daniels?"

They all chose their respective shots.

"You know what they say about shots," Melissa said cheekily. "One's fine, two's the most, three under the table, four under the host ... or hosts." She winked at Brian as his face turned red.

She is bold as brass, he thought. *Shit, can I really do this?*

They all shared a laugh as they clinked shot glasses.

"So ... " Sarah cleared her throat nervously. "Pardon my asking, but do you do this often?" She leveled the question at Travis, while sizing him up. *He is very good looking, damn!*

And he was! 6 foot 2, amazing muscular shoulders, thick, wavy dark hair, sensuous brown eyes, just enough scruff on his face to make him look sexy as hell! She felt her body responding to him already.

"No, not really," he returned in a low, rich voice. "Maybe a few times a year. We're not whores. We're clean people, we just like a little spice once in a while." He smirked charmingly.

A few more shots were downed, conversation started to flow more easily, and everyone started to relax and enjoy themselves.

Brian eyeballed Melissa. She was highly attractive, as well. Long blonde hair, ample bosom, quite petite.

She's not going to want to sleep with me, he thought, getting dejected.

Melissa caught him ogling her and smiled seductively. "So, do we want to take things to the next level tonight or was this just a meet and greet?" She looked around at the group. "Or anyone want to back out?"

"You don't beat around the bush, do you?" Brian teased her.

She laughed playfully. "No, I am pretty direct." Her eyes bored into his.

He felt his body react. *Hoo boy! Here we go.*

Sarah and Travis gazed at each other intensely. "Let's play," said Travis.

Melissa and Brian retreated to the master bedroom, his bedroom with his wife. He felt a little tinge of anxiety ripple through his body at the thought of having sex on his marriage bed with another woman. But also, it was kind of a turn on. The thought of his wife having sex with some strange hot guy down the hall also passed through his mind and made him a little jealous and upset but he did agree to this.

At least they're not next door, I don't want to hear it, he thought. *This was a bad idea.* He blew out a long breath.

He stood at the sliding glass door, watching the moon play on the lake, facing away from Melissa.

She could tell he was nervous. She went to him and massaged his shoulders. "Relax, we can ease into this," she said softly. "Lie down on the bed — I'll give you a massage."

"Alright," Brian replied, as she took his hand and led him to the bed. She unbuttoned his shirt and let it drop to the floor. She reached for the button on his jeans and he put his hand over hers, stopping her.

"Let me do it, please," she purred into his ear. "I think you look great." She massaged the front of his trousers.

He inhaled sharply and let her undo his jeans, then he laid down on the bed and turned on to his stomach, happy to hide his somewhat rotund belly from this beautiful woman.

"Now ... relax." She stripped down to her thong underwear and unlatched her bra. Her generous breasts spilled out.

Brian felt her straddle him, she gently rubbed her tight bottom over his.

"Good God," he breathed, feeling a mixture of pleasure and embarrassment.

She moved to his shoulders, gently squeezing and making soft circling motions, and moved inward.

"Nice."

She continued rubbing and kneading his back. She could feel him starting to finally loosen up. Her breasts softly rubbed against his back, gently back and forth.

He moaned softly. He was really getting into it. He moved and flipped into a seated position.

She sat on his lap. She could feel his erect manhood pressing against her inner thigh through his underwear.

They shared a few soft, tender kisses, then started to go deeper, harder, longer. She playfully sucked on his top lip.

He moved to her neck, planting soft kisses down to her full breasts, then lightly caressed her breasts. She moaned softly, rubbing her body against his as he gently kissed and sucked on her erect nipple.

She eased his underwear off and grasped his hard member, slowly, rubbing her thumb up and down the shaft. He felt alive and electric. He couldn't take much more as he grabbed her lower back and eased her onto his penis.

He exhaled sharply as she rode him slowly, then increased tempo. It was so intense, exciting and new that he couldn't last overly long, and he climaxed fast and hard.

"That was amazing," he gasped, his breathing labored. He looked a little embarrassed. "I'm sorry I was a little quick. You are just so beautiful and sexy as hell." He kissed her lightly.

She let out a sensuous laugh. "I'm glad you enjoyed it."

He rubbed his bald head. "Whoo! Now that we got the first-time nervousness over ... " He gave her a saucy look. "And now that I'm relaxed ... let me make it up to you."

He positioned himself on top of her and gave her body a slow, scintillating going over with his hands, mouth, and tongue. He felt like a new man as he listened to her sigh and squeal. It made him feel recharged and confident again as she writhed and cried out as he made her come with his mouth.

In the other room, things were quite the opposite. There wasn't any self-consciousness going on. Things got hot and heavy pretty fast.

Sarah was completely thrilled and turned on by being with a younger, hot man. She loved her husband, but it was amazing to be with someone completely opposite — hot bod, gorgeous thick hair, mega stamina!

They explored each other's bodies eagerly and easily, crazily switching positions like porn stars. They both peaked as they did it doggy-style while he massaged her sweet spot.

"Oh my God," Sarah exclaimed breathlessly as they lay entwined in the afterglow. "Just — oh my God!"

He let out a low, goose bump causing sexy laugh. "I know." He slowly caressed her thigh.

After a while, they all emerged from the bedrooms and sat down in the living room for a glass of wine and some snacks. All of them had cheeky grins on their faces.

These romps became a once a week affair, and things became bolder every time. A bit of bondage — and some toys were even introduced.

As it happens, Brian was best friends way back in grade school with David Blake, the man across the lake. They both were able to stay on the lake pretty much their whole lives, with properties being passed down. They would regularly tool around the lake in Brian's party boat, without the wives.

As they lazily made their way around the lake one hot summer afternoon, David couldn't help but notice Brian grinning like a Cheshire cat.

"You're very chipper today," he commented.

Brian chuckled. "I'm in a great mood, best I felt in years."

Dave nodded. "Good for you. No middle age crisis bogging you down?"

He swigged his beer. "Actually, my wife's middle age crisis has boosted my life immensely." He laughed again.

Dave crinkled his eyes. "What? Don't keep me in suspense," he probed good-naturedly.

"I really shouldn't say anything, but hell I've known you my whole life ... " His blue eyes danced as he looked at his friend who sat there expectantly.

"We've been swinging," he blurted out proudly.

Dave's head went back. "Are you serious?" He was incredulous.

"Yeah — for quite a while now." He drank his beer again. "What a goddamned rush! I never knew I was so good in bed! I have this hot, young little number going crazy for it."

He looked at his friend from top to bottom. He couldn't believe it. *I sound like a catty woman!* he thought and laughed. "Your wife initiated it?"

"I couldn't believe it either." He shook his head wondrously. "I was dubious because ... well ... you know ... look at me." He laughed.

So did Dave. "Good to know some women are into a little diversity," he said kindly.

He filled him in on all the sizzling details as they cracked open two more beers and motored around the lake one more time.

"So fat Brian is swinging," Dave delightedly informed his wife. "Can you believe it?"

Samantha's eyebrows shot up. "For real?" She twisted her face up.

"Oh yeah. I believe him. Why make it up?" He shrugged his shoulders. "Even named the couple. They are also on the lake."

She made a surprised sound. "This lake is a hotbed of sex, drugs and intrigue." She giggled.

"Indeed."

They sat on their deck with a cocktail and watched the array of lake traffic glide by while he entertained her with this titillating bit of gossip.

Surer than hell, fantasy doesn't last too long, and a cold slap of reality hit Brian hard in the face when he came home one day to find his wife had packed her bags and high-tailed it out of his life to shack up with her new, young, chiseled lover. Two marriages shattered!

He sat on the couch, his head in his hands, shell-shocked, reading her terse note. "A goddamned note! I get a flipping note!" he yelled to the quiet house. "Twenty-one years!" He phoned Melissa, but she didn't pick up. He tried over and over — nothing. "Sonofabitch!" he snarled.

Chapter 5

Get Sewing Mama!

The lake was beautiful this morning as Pat Smith gazed out the kitchen window and made his coffee. He was a coffee connoisseur and loved *the wine of the bean*. A few years back, he had attended a coffee cupping lab in NYC where he enjoyed sampling the different roasts of ground beans. At the lab, Pat had enjoyed sampling the many types of roasted coffee beans. He loved the detailed procedure, the 4-minute brew, scooping away the crusty grains at the top of the cup, slurping it down while savoring every drop. He could now determine the country of origin from just a few sniffs of the brew.

He selected the lighter roasted, Arabica beans for the maximum dose of caffeine that he needed today and turned the grinder on. A macchiato was what he needed and began to prepare. He was ready for the day before him, coffee first, a leisurely soak in the hot tub, a few laps in the pool perhaps and then off to work.

Pat was a wealthy entrepreneur. He ran a coffee import business into New England but a few years back, he began doing a little more than importing coffee. He had expanded the business from coffee to a more lucrative product, drugs. Pat had issues with what he considered the hard-core drugs like heroin or fentanyl and refused to get into that market. He left that to the Mexicans and the mob as he did not want to be responsible for any overdoses or deaths. His preference was for drugs like cocaine and MDMA or Ecstasy.

The club scene in Boston was thriving and he had a considerable clientele right at his fingertips in the neighborhood. His partying neighbors were always tooling around on their boats, high as kites and demanding more and more of his goods.

Pat's meanderings stopped as his wife Lily entered the kitchen.

"A penny for your thoughts?" she asked.

"Just thinking about work. Nothing interesting," he replied as he shifted his weight, irritated by his wife's prodding. He needed his morning coffee, and pronto!

"Ah, that again. Gets in the way of a lot of things." She brushed by him gracefully attending to their three Great Danes who bounded up the stairs barking loudly.

It was really Lily that was indirectly responsible for their affluent lifestyle. Control of the coffee business was given to Lily after she and Pat married. Lily's dad had passed when she was a young girl and her mother became quickly fed up running the complex organization, so she signed over the company making Pat, CEO and Lily, CFO. They had four children quickly in succession, who now as adults, were involved in Pat's expansion of the company.

Michael walked into the kitchen. "Hey Mom, Pops, any coffee?"

He was their oldest son and graduated from law school. He lived in the house next-door and continually popped in and out. He dealt with the money side of things, laundering revenues from their more recent cocaine enterprise and other financial matters that came up from bribes to police or politicians, to clerical bookkeeping matters. Wherever money was involved, Michael was the overseer. He was quiet and usually withdrawn but passionate about company finances and an asset to their business. His law expertise and tax knowledge had saved them millions.

"Sure, pull up a chair," Lily responded as she ground up some more coffee beans.

"Can't beat that smell of freshly brewed coffee! Got some extra for me?" yelled Mark as he strode down the hallway to join his parents and brother.

Mark was the second oldest. He was certainly not the bookkeeping type like his older brother. Handsome and athletic, he spent every hour outdoors. He had a master license in boating and held a private pilot license. If he wasn't driving a boat, he was behind it, waterskiing or barefoot skiing, and if he wasn't piloting a plane, he was sky diving out of one.

"I thought we were having a meeting. Where is Marianne and Jeff?" Mark asked about his two missing siblings, Marianne being the youngest.

His enthusiasm was contagious. Pat would have to put off that hot tub dip. He had forgotten about their breakfast meeting.

"Hello, hello we're here!" Marianne and Jeff burst in the front door and headed to the kitchen. Marianne drifted in, her beauty reflecting in everyone's eyes, except for her father's. Pat had not yet come to terms with his daughter's recent coming out. He was old-school, and this LGBTQ thing was nonsense to him. His youngest son, Jeff stood beside her.

"How's everyone this fine morning?" Jeff asked of his family. "How's it going Pops?"

"Fine son, fine," replied Pat.

Pat was most proud of his youngest son, his great hulking body towered over Marianne. Jeff was the black sheep of the family, or that is what they humorously called him. His musculature and build gave away his position in the family business. He was head of security and dealt with the company's operational details like a black ops mission. Security, guns, ammunition, and communication were under his command.

"Coffee time!" said Lily. "Come on, let's all sit down."

It was just 9 o'clock as Lily looked around at her children and smiled at Pat. She was grateful to him for keeping her children close to home. Pat had built a house for each of his children on the cul-de-sac they called home. People who turned down their road were family or friends only, and that is the way they liked it.

"I made some pancakes and waffles, eat up!" Lily brought over a huge plate and set it down in front of her family.

"Yum, my favorite, blueberry pancakes." Marianne smiled gratefully at her mother. "Thanks Mom."

Her brothers chimed in with appreciative agreement.

"OK," said Pat, "so where do we stand with this new opportunity with Leo in Venezuela? What did you find out?" He nodded to his youngest sons.

At this question, Mark and Jeffrey both perked up. They had just returned the day before from their meeting with Leo in Venezuela.

"Mark got us down there no problem. From here to Florida to the Bahamas and then to Venezuela. It was clear sailing if you can say that about flying!" Jeff grinned at his own pun and looked at Mark.

"Yeah, it was a smooth flight. We found the airstrip no problem, with their GPS coordinates," said Mark. "It was in a small jungle clearing. After landing, we were surrounded by Leo's armed guerillas in five jeeps. It was kind of crazy. But Jeff took care of that end."

"Once they figured out who we were and saw my AK47 they calmed down considerably." Jeff's voice was animated. "They drove us to the hacienda. It was 15 minutes away, through dense jungle terrain."

Mark interjected, "Leo greeted us at the hacienda and gave us a tour. He has a whole community living with him. He even has a petting zoo full of animals for the little kids!" Mark's love for animals was an accepted fact in the family.

Pat smiled at his middle son, thinking that he was always too soft on him and nodded at Jeff. "So the operation? Is it feasible? What's your gut tell you?"

Mark squirmed in his seat trying to hide his feelings of disappointment as his father seemed to care more about Jeff's opinion. He stuffed himself with some more waffles.

Jeff became official and business-like. "Leo's operation seems fairly tight. He has five huge warehouses for the harvested coco leaves, a separate warehouse for processing the paste and another for converting it into the final product. There's a small army of workers and guards in the compound. He wants to cut out the handling of the shipment by the ports as its costing him too much to pay off everybody."

Mark couldn't contain himself any longer and jumped in, "I don't know about this. This guy thinks he's king of the world and we are his servants. He offered me the services of a few women on the compound and some heroin too. It's all too much for us. I didn't like his attitude." Mark was lying about the heroin, but he knew his father's opinion on the matter.

"Heroin! You know that's not where we are going! And be careful about any women down there," Pat stated vehemently.

"Yeah Pops we know. There's no heroin involved in the shipment. It's all cocaine and some 'E'," Jeff retorted, "I think we could be into something good here. It's manageable. I have a good feeling about this one. I say, it's a go."

Pat looked at Jeff regarding him thoughtfully. He was the muscle needed for the operation. His senses usually paid off and Pat respected his advice. Pat looked from Jeff to his wife and daughter who were leaning into the conversation while Michael remained stoic as usual.

"If we go ahead with this, it will require that everyone is on board with it." Pat eyed Mark. "What about the logistics with the plane and boat Mark? Is it doable?" Pat knew he had to get Mark on board or else the deal would fail.

Mark suddenly realized that his father wanted this deal to go down. He had to go along with it, but at least he felt valued now, so he expressed only his positive thoughts.

"Leo and his men can handle it. Operationally, they have a Cessna 310 which they can load up with 500 kilos of product and fly it to Exumas. Then dump the plane without damaging the load of course. Jeff and I will boat over, get the product, and head straight over to the Bahamas, to our plane. It"ll be a piece of cake really, Pops!" Mark smiled at his aging father.

"We'll be back in no time. Then we can bring our load to our darling little sis for packaging and processing for our hungry consumers." Jeff joined in happily and smiled at Marianne. "I gave Leo a phone for all future communications with us. And said we'd be in contact if the deal was a go."

Jeff had given the whole family a set of these special phones for the business. The phones were impenetrable to police wiretapping, or requests from judicial agencies for phone logs as they had all apps, texting, internet and GPS capabilities removed. It was provided by Casper Security, a no frills, private, encrypted network for the underworld.

"I told Leo, like I told you guys, these phones are our lifeline for any business activity. I don't need to remind you that if you lose your phone or the police get it, you need to contact me immediately and I'll notify Casper and get the phone locked down," Jeff stated with authority.

"Yeah, yeah, you told us before," Mark said. His brother was irritating him about this phone thing again. "And we can just hit *9, and our emails disappear, we get it! We're not stupid!"

"OK, boys settle down." Lily sensed the sibling rivalry and competition for their father's attention in her two younger sons.

"No worries, no hassles, Mom," Jeff replied. "In summary, I think it's a go." He smiled broadly at his father.

Jeff's mind dwelled on all the other potential assets of the network phones, which he neglected to tell his family members. It included Casper Security's client list of over 20,000 users all over the continental US, South America, Australia, Thailand and Hong Kong. E-mail accounts detailed services for the criminal community like 'dialahit@casper.com,' 'cartel@casper.com,' '24hourlaundry@casper.com,' and 'wecleanup4U@caspercom.' To date, the family had not needed these services, but the new expansion might require such a potential workforce. *These contacts would be useful in the future,* he thought to himself, *especially if this deal with Leo is a go. It's a whole new dimension.*

"What say you Marianne?" Jeff asked of his sister.

Marianne ran the packaging and processing of the final product when it finally got to Massachusetts. She had an office and lab set up with a staff of 30 in a nearby church facility. Its cover was a local nonprofit for economically challenged women called 'Go Girls Now.' With her college chemistry degree, Marianne ran the nonprofit and the lab with immense success and the community support was overwhelming.

"I see no problem," she stated confidently, "the girls and I will easily be able to manage that amount of new product. Just so long as you tell me the distribution volumes you want. It will be fine. We can handle whatever you throw at us. If I must hire more girls, I will."

Lily looked over at her daughter, admiring her confidence with this new task and wondering about her sexuality. Pat was so totally against Marianne's recently proclaimed sexual lifestyle that she felt the need to support her daughter, but her heart was not quite in it. Marianne was beautiful, intelligent and caring. Although she accepted her daughter's choice, inwardly, Lily cried over the loss of future grandkids.

"That's great, Marianne," Pat said. "Okay, you're the only one left Michael. What do you think?" Pat asked of his eldest son, the head of finances, Michael. He had been quiet until now except for the occasional clicking of his pen, a habit he couldn't rid himself of when he was contemplating matters.

"Right! It seems to me like all you guys have done your homework," Michael thoughtfully replied. "I have been working through the numbers. From my calculations, I estimate that by taking out any middle men at the port, a 500-kilo transit, would cost around $1.5 million and would bring in anywhere from $12-75 million dependent on quantities for distribution. So, the profit margin is in your hands Mom and Sis! But this looks like a deal with immense potential and very, very lucrative."

His pen clicking had reached a climax by the time he had finished speaking. Michael was straight and to the point, just like his father, no mincing of words. But that pen clicking had to stop! Pat was just going to explode when Michael abruptly stopped clicking and talking.

"Well, I'd better get moving then!" Lily jumped up and began to clear the table.

Her movements signaled an end to the meeting. She had no interest in the details of the new business direction but enjoyed her recent creative participation in it. She loved to sew and had started a small business making handbags to sell at craft shows. Her artistry expanded from handbags to backpacks, clutches and phone totes. The business grew exponentially when she began including secret compartments for drugs and paraphernalia. The target market was the rich clubgoers and partygoers, weddings, baby showers, birthdays, bachelorette or bachelor parties. It was a niche market of sorts, but supply and demand was up in recent months as word of mouth spread. With the inclusion of the final product, Lily envisioned her workload escalating dramatically.

"If we have a little more diversity of our product, it will definitely improve business, don't you think Marianne?" Lily asked.

"Yes, for sure. If we put a gram of product in every bag, well … that's the minimum and maybe up the amount in the bride's bag to 5 grams, that may get anywhere from \$200 to \$2000, … depending on quality and choice of product. Don't you think Michael?"

"Sounds like a viable idea. I'll run the numbers." Michael scratched away on paper.

"Business will be booming!" Lily exclaimed. "I have some new designs I want to get going on. I am ready and willing!"

"So, it's a go then, next week. Make it happen!" Pat summed up the meeting. "Jeff, you contact Leo, and Mark make sure the boat and plane are ready. Michael run the numbers for your sister and Marianne set about getting some new girls in for the extra work."

Pat got up to get ready for his hot tub and swim. "Now off with all you guys. I have to go to work!" He laughed heartily and headed off for his daily relaxation.

"Bye! Pops and Mom, love you both!" Marianne exclaimed as she readied herself to head to her office and her loyal female staff.

"Bye darling," Lily hugged her daughter affectionately. "Give us a kiss, boys!" Lily demanded of her three sons who dutifully responded with a kiss on the cheek and murmured their goodbyes. She walked them to the door while restraining the dogs from galloping out.

"Join me in the tub?" Pat called out.

"No thanks, I have a lot of sewing to do with this new increase in market volume," she jokingly said.

"Do me a favor and call that brother-in-law of yours at the DEA and poke around. See if he knows anything or has any information about this Leo B guy in Venezuela."

"Sure," she replied.

Lily's sister had married a DEA agent which came in useful sometimes. It was good to have inside knowledge if possible. She went into the parlor, dialed and got her brother-in-law, Zach.

"Hi, Zach, it's me. Is Rose there?" Lily tried to be offhand in her conversation.

"No, she's out shopping as usual," Zach replied.

"Oh, that's a shame. Just calling to chat." Lily dove right into the main reason for her call. "How's your FBI/DEA stuff doing? Any news about our lake?"

"Yeah," Zach replied, "we are ramping up. We have another house now, towards the southern end. The house at the north end of the lake was too remote to be of much surveillance use, all those trees block everything out. There's a Spanish family and a group of Paddy's, with possible terrorist connections we're watching. You know anything about them?"

"Nothing about Irish terrorists," said Lily feeding him information, "but there's been talk all over the neighborhood about the Spanish guy. The locals suspect gun running, illegal immigrants, sex parties, heroin dealing and even human trafficking. The rumors are just flowing."

"Is that right?" said Zach letting his sister in-law run off her mouth as usual.

She continued, "A guy named Victor seems to be the head of the family. He has a lot of money flowing around him, and bought several houses on the lake. Some he rents out and others he keeps for himself. Everything he buys, he pays for in cash," she added.

"Is that right?" Zach replied again while he wondered if Lily picked up on his bored tone of voice.

Lily elaborated further, "He trades in his ski boat every year for a new one." She felt a little awkward relaying some of this information to Zach, but it was only gossip. "They even built a huge garage and filled it with Ferraris and Porsches. Some people say he won the lottery, or he is a hedge fund manager or a banker for junk bonds. Maybe he's a drug dealer or a gun runner? I don't know really, I thought you might?" She paused as she waited for him to fill in any gaps.

"Well you know the local police has heard many complaints from neighbors on the lake and now the state police are investigating a ring that's bringing heroin up from New York and supplying all of New England. Maybe there's a connection?"

"Oh wow, do you think?" said Lily.

"The ring drives up the interstate from NY and makes stops in Connecticut, and Massachusetts before they hit New Hampshire, Vermont and Maine." Zach paused for a second. He might be sharing too much with his sister-in-law. FBI informers had said there was a new distributor of heroin living on the lake, possibly linked to the Italian Mob and Victor Santiago. Zach already knew about the cash sales of houses in the area and the stretch of property the Santiago family now owned. The local police had numerous complaints about the Irish terrorist group who were under surveillance. "That's about it Lily." Zach decided to keep his tongue in check.

"Are the drugs coming up from South America then? Mexico, Columbia or maybe Venezuela?" Lily persisted. "I heard there were new guys in charge of the cartel down in southern parts. Some guy called Leo?" she pushed Zach further than she wanted.

"No. Looks like that's kind of dried up now with Escobar gone," Zach replied. "How's the kids and Pat?" Zach asked, changing topics. His sister-in-law was much too interested in his work all the time. It was beginning to bore and annoy him answering her prying questions.

"Oh, they were all here for breakfast. Everyone's great. Tell Rose I'll call her later then. Talk soon!"

"OK. I'll tell Rose you called, say hi to Pat for me." Zach ended the call.

Lily went to find Pat and relay the conversation.

"Sorry Pat. There's no real news from Zach," Lily said over the circulating jets of the hot tub. "He said they are currently focused on a ring out of New York, possibly mob related and that guy Victor. He also mentioned an Irish group who might be involved in something or other and another FBI house on the lake. That's all I got from him. Hey, it's getting a little hot around here, don't you think?" She smiled at him. *He was still in great shape*, she thought.

"That's fine, now come on Lily, join me before I go to work?" Pat said as he winked at her.

Lily slipped off her clothes quickly and joined her husband in the hot tub, giggling like a school girl and sliding in beside him.

After Marianne left her parent's house, said goodbye to her brothers, she headed to work. She toyed with the idea of visiting some friends she had just met on the lake. After all, she was the boss, and it really didn't matter if she was in late. She had supervised the hiring of all her staff and they were loyal to their leader. She demanded excellence and in turn rewarded her staff for their efforts. All her girls were amazing and were well capable of running the operation without her.

She veered off the main road and headed to the small A-frame house. Her new friends were Irish natives. She was unsure if they were illegal immigrants or not but what she was sure of was, they were fun. She had only begun hanging out with them and was thoroughly enjoying their youthful disregard of anything normal. They were loud, noisy, pot smoking hippies, possibly heroin dealers and/or addicts according to the surrounding neighbors. She smiled as she remembered the wizened neighbor next door threatening action against them as she waved her pointy witch-like finger toward them, calling them every name she could drum up as they laughed back in her face.

Marianne parked her car and approached the house. Her new friends, Bridget and Alice lived there with 4 guys, Martin, Tommy, Joe and Mickey. Marianne loved hearing their Irish accents which were totally distinct and different, as they hailed from differing parts of the small island. They had the life in Marianne's opinion as they could all work from the A-frame house in the summer, telecommuting for their new software company.

The Irish group were a bunch of partiers and revelers. They were always singing, playing music, dancing and enjoying the lake on their jet skis, and rafts. They had anti-British slogans decorating the house, 'Don't Do it Megan,' protesting the upcoming royal marriage of Prince Harry and Megan Markel. Motorbikes and jet skis dominated the driveway and surrounding available space. They infrequently used hard drugs but drank like fish and there was always a full bowl of homegrown pot on the kitchen table.

A new sign greeted her at the door, an anti-Trump one. *That's going to drum up the neighbors*, thought Marianne smiling as she rang the doorbell. She was greeted by all 6 people as the door opened.

"Hiya! You're not the FBI or the police? Come on in!" said Bridget who was first at the door. "You're never going to believe this."

Marianne was ushered into the kitchen and they all sat around while Joe rolled up a giant joint, lit it and began to pass it around. Cups of tea and biscuits littered the table.

"We had a dawn raid by the FBI," Bridget began, "at 6 AM when the doorbell rang. I wasn't up but Mickey and Tommy were up as their 2 friends, Kevin and James arrived in the early hours from Florida. Sorry forgot to introduce you. Marianne, this is Kevin and James." They all nodded hi to each other.

"Mickey opened the door and the FBI barged in, grabbed him and pushed him to the floor, yelling 'FBI don't move, on the ground and show us your hands!' " Bridget mimicked their authoritative voices.

"Yeah it was kind of terrifying really. They grabbed me and told me to get on the floor, guns drawn and all." Mickey dramatically pointed his finger into Marianne's face.

"There was 8 of them. They rushed into the kitchen and found Kevin and James and pushed them to the floor and then went room to room screaming, 'FBI, get on the floor, shut up and put your hands over your heads.' It was like out of a fucking TV show!" Mickey laughed about the incident, the pot taking hold of his brain.

"They interrogated each of us, in our rooms and then brought us into the kitchen. 'Okay we have them all, bring them into the kitchen!' one cop said." Tommy parodied the head FBI agent.

"Oh my God, what a nightmare. No thanks!" said Marianne passing the joint to Bridget.

"Let me tell you what happened to me," jumped in Alice.

Of the 2 women Marianne had a special fondness for Alice although Bridget was also incredibly attractive in her own rights.

Alice continued excitedly telling her story. "I heard the commotion at the door and immediately thought *it's the landlord, hide!* I heard a male voice bark 'How many of them are there?' so I jumped up right out of bed and hopped into the closet. I thought it was the fucking landlord! Then I heard 'FBI no one move!' and I thought, *Crap it's the FBI and I'm hiding in a fucking closet! What am I going to do? They'll fucking shoot me. They'll never believe me.* I heard them come into my room. I waited for a while and listened carefully. Not hearing any sound, I crept out of the closet. But shit, there was a fucking FBI guy in my room, with his back to me. 'Hi,' I said. He twisted around and pulled out his gun. 'Don't move!' Fortunately, I was naked, I think or else he would have shot me." Alice laughed uncontrollably, the pot encouraging her levity.

"He was just gazing at your pretty eyes, and you disarmed him," said Tommy laughing with her.

"You're right, Tommy! But that's not all he was looking at!" Alice retorted. "Then I started telling him how I thought he was the landlord and I was not really Irish but American. I couldn't stop laughing as I watched his gaze go to the anti-Brit poster on the wall. Can you fucking imagine I was hiding in a closet during an FBI raid, what the fuck?" She looked at Marianne for her reaction.

"That sounds crazy! You lunatic, hiding in a closet!" said Marianne.

"He told me to get dressed and he'd send in a female agent to interview me. I told her the same landlord story and then she brought me into the kitchen with the others," Alice said.

"I thought that they were telling each other jokes or something the way that Alice was laughing. You could hear her in the fucking kitchen," said Martin.

"Give me a fucking break, Martin. I was just nervous. I laugh when I'm nervous," Alice said. "The bowl of pot was sitting right on the table, but the FBI ignored it. They wanted to know if we had anything else, like heroin or guns! Can you fucking believe it?"

Bridget interrupted Alice's stream of talk. "I offered them all a cup of tea which they declined. 'Are you afraid it's poisoned?' I asked them. And they sniggered and said that we were just small fish in a much larger fishing pond and left as quickly as they came."

"What a nightmare!" said Marianne.

"Yep. Unbelievable right? Can you imagine, us terrorists? Illegal immigrants maybe, terrorists no!" Alice laughed again. "But wait, it's not over. After a few cups of tea and a few jays to calm us down, the doorbell rang again. This time I got up to answer the door jokingly saying, 'they're back!' When I opened the door more fucking police! They pushed me up against the wall and stormed the house again. With everyone in the kitchen they didn't have to go too far."

"Who is Kevin Peter Murphy? they yelled. So, Kevin here says, 'I'm Kevin Alan Murphy and this is my brother James Peter Murphy. There's no fucking Kevin Peter Murphy here.' They looked at our passports saw the FBI's mistake and left saying 'the FBI didn't know their arse from their elbow!' Funny eh?" Alice took another hit from the joint.

"And we've all been here ever since. Having a few cups of lovely poisoned tea, right Bridget?" said Martin.

"And a few biscuits to go with our tea too," Tommy laughingly said.

"I would have loved to put some pot in their tea," chimed in Bridget. "They'd be high FBI!" She chuckled at her rhyme. "High FBI get it?" The pot was kicking in nicely for her.

"You could have been our third raid of the day and it's not even 10!" Alice tittered at Marianne, "Although you don't look scary to me!" She went to Marianne and gave her a big hug.

"Hey, I'll have some of that!" Bridget joined in their hug.

"Any chance of expanding that group hug here?" asked Martin.

"What you think?" said Alice as the three women left the kitchen and headed towards her bedroom. Alice raised her hand behind the women's backs in an appropriate one finger salute to the onlooking men.

Chapter 6

Don't Drink and Float

In one of the most palatial and gorgeous houses on the lake, Estelle Gray lives, a retired teacher. The house has so many windows and is so huge, it looks like a hotel. She and her second husband Luke, live there, the kids are all grown up and out on their own.

Empty nest syndrome and retirement have taken a massive toll on her. Ennui has settled in. To cope with the utter boredom, Estelle has been hitting the bottle, pretty hard.

She barely eats, just lays in bed and drinks most of the time. She looks ghastly, skeletal thin, and even her husband is growing weary of it.

"See you later, Estelle, I'm going fishing," he called to her as she sat up in bed, polishing off a bottle of vodka.

"Ha! I'm sure you are," she sneered. "Do have fun." *You asshole*, she thought.

She knew where he was going — to get a 'massage' from some cheap slut on the lake — who did more than massage for the right price. She may be the lake sot, but she wasn't oblivious to anything, she knew every juicy tidbit and scandal on the body of water. And when she was three sheets to the wind, like a lot of drinkers, she had no filter, got obnoxious, blunt, and let her mouth run and say whatever she damn well felt.

One beautiful summer afternoon, as usual Estelle was passed out on the couch.

Her husband nudged her. "Get up! The Turners are here in their party boat. We have to keep up appearances once in a while," he grumbled. "Can you get up?"

She put her arm on her forehead and sighed. "Yeah, yeah ... I can get up." She slowly rose off the couch.

They made their way down their yard. She stumbled a bit stepping onto the dock.

"She's been at it already," someone snidely remarked in a hushed tone.

People smirked knowingly.

Her husband helped her onto the boat, she was a bit unsteady.

"Hello, everyone!" she greeted.

"Hi, Estelle," several voices responded.

They convivially tooled around the lake, several libations were consumed, everyone was chit-chatting.

"Oh Kathy, I was so sorry to hear of your husband's passing," one lady sympathetically remarked.

"Thank you, it has been difficult."

"Yes, I'm sure," Estelle piped up. "How many has this been? Two? Three?"

"Just one," Kathy disdainfully replied.

"Ah — indeed." Estelle sipped her wine. "What bad luck — you poor thing."

The boat was hushed in shocked silence.

Kathy's eyes were icy slits. "Just what are you implying? I had something to do with it?" she huffed. "He drowned, you ignorant harpy!"

"Now, now ladies."

Estelle wasn't one to back down. "You poor dear ... you should meet Earl down the lake —" She drunkenly pointed. "He lost his wife — and at least two or three girlfriends after that. You could see which one outlasts the other," she sneered.

Kathy gasped, as did others.

"Estelle!" her husband barked. "Enough!"

She rolled her eyes. "Whatever."

"Sorry everybody," Luke apologized, sheepishly looking around. "We need to go home. Sorry we ruined your afternoon."

Back at their house, Estelle was once again on the couch, vodka bottle in hand.

Her incensed husband stood over her, shaking his head. "For Christ sake, Estelle, do you always have to make an ass out of yourself and embarrass the shit out of me?" he chastised, thoroughly disgusted. "You need to get some help."

She took another swig of the hooch. "Aaah!" She laid her head back on the cushion. "Then divorce me." She looked at him with glazed eyes. "Oh yeah, this is my house and I have all the money," she mercilessly harassed him.

He rolled his eyes. "You are so pitiful." He agitatedly rubbed his face and sighed heavily. "I don't need to do that. I just have to wait a little while longer and you'll drink yourself to death," he vengefully needled her and let out a harsh laugh.

"Good. At this point there isn't much to keep me going." She lifted up the bottle. "At least this breaks up the endless tedium." She closed her eyes.

"Go for it," he ground out. "Bottoms up, you pathetic lush." With that, he left the room and slammed the front door.

One July afternoon, the weather was sweltering, so she decided to go float around on the lake. By herself of course, as few people could stand her. With her cocktail placed firmly in an indentation in the raft, she blissfully floated around in the sun.

Then she fell asleep.

As the powerful inboard came from around the ski jump in the middle of the lake, whilst pulling a jumper, the driver noticed a hot pink raft smack dab in front of him, not too far away. He was roaring at top speed, and barely had time to jerk the wheel hard to the side and veer out of the way.

"Holy shit! You idiot!" he yelled as he sped by.

Estelle was still oblivious.

The harsh jerking of the rope was enough to make the jumper completely wipe out, so he also started yelling angrily. "Nice way to get yourself killed, you fool!" he bit out as the boat circled back to pick him up.

Estelle was still in her alcoholic stupor, unaware of the commotion around her. Finally, the rocking of the waves against her raft pitched her into the water. The shock of the cold water jarred her awake. She started flailing in the water and couldn't get back on the float. She was in trouble.

Angus McGregor, one of the nicest and most jovial people on the lake, who enjoys taking anyone who wants to go for a ride on his party boat, and who never holds a grudge about anyone, witnessed the whole scene and raced to rescue her.

He zoomed up beside her. "Hang on, Estelle! We got you!" he assured her.

"Help me!"

Two male passengers managed to grab her by the arms and hoisted her on board. One of them grabbed her raft, as well.

"Are you OK?" Angus asked.

Estelle was still kind of foggy. "Yeah, I'm OK — I'm so sorry. I must've fallen asleep."

I'm sure, Angus sarcastically thought. "You need to be careful — tether yourself to your dock or something," he seriously suggested.

"I know, thank you."

They helped her on to her dock and made sure she made it into her house.

Angus shook his head. "That poor lady — she really has a problem."

"I hear you had another incident," her husband mocked, shaking his head.

"So what. You weren't there to be mortified about it."

"True. But I still have to hear about how my wife is the boozed-up laughing stock of the lake."

"I'll say it again — get out then!"

"I'm seriously considering it."

The Y Camp was having their annual summer bash, and all were invited.

When Luke and Estelle walked in, a few heads turned and there was some murmuring amongst the crowd.

Some people quaked in their boots when she showed up at places, hoping they weren't the next to be 'outed' so to speak by her vicious tongue and candid comments, hoping their secrets were safe. But other people enjoyed hearing her blast people for their misdeeds and learning all the new gossip about the lake residents.

Things were going well, they mingled affably with people that they knew. A few drinks were quaffed. Estelle was behaving herself, everyone was delighted. Until she spied the woman who gave out the 'massages' on the lake, Heather Drake.

Estelle made a beeline for the woman and got right in her face.

"So, how's the massage business going?" Her voice dripped with vitriol. "How many men do you service— oops — I mean massage? Knowing all the lecherous men around here, you probably screw half the lake," she snidely accused.

Heather gasped.

Estelle jabbed her finger in Heather's face. "I know my husband is one. You're not getting anything over on me, you dirty tramp," she snarled.

Heather looked shell-shocked. "What the hell are you talking about?"

Estelle let out a short laugh. "Oh, please. Everyone knows you're a whore."

"You alcoholic bitch!" Heather threw her glass of wine in Estelle's face. "There, have another drink!"

Heads turned, and the crowd grew silent as they listened to the brouhaha as it continued.

Estelle slapped her. "You hussy!" She wiped the wine off her face. "Frankly, I don't really give a damn, you can have him — he's always been lousy in bed!"

There were some titters among the crowd.

Luke came storming over. "What the hell is going on over here?" he angrily asked, interrupting the shouting match. He pulled his wife away from Heather.

"My God, must you always make a damned scene?" His eyes bored into his wife. "Enough of this. I've had enough!" His tone was gruff as he harshly led his wife out of the party, as all eyes watch this sordid scenario.

Estelle jerked her arm away. "Don't manhandle me!" she seethed.

"Just zip it," he ordered as they disappeared up the forest path and made their way to the parking lot.

In the private confines of the automobile, he tore into her.

"That's it, Estelle, I'm so done with this." He exhaled a disgusted breath. "I could tell you to go to a program, I'm sure you wouldn't." He paused, wearily rubbing his forehead. "I don't give a shit what you do anymore. I'm out ... I'm leaving. I don't have to put up with this torture anymore, living on pins and needles, wondering when you'll go off again."

He started the car and peeled out of the parking lot.

"Good," she hissed out. "When are you going?"

"Tomorrow. My brother said I could stay with him."

"I'm sure," she said sardonically.

"I don't care what you think. This marriage has been crumbling for years. You're married to the vodka bottle, not me," he bitterly told her.

She was passed out in the passenger seat.

He looked at her in utter contempt and disenchantment. "That figures." He pursed his lips and drove home in silence.

With her husband estranged and moved out, Estelle became even worse. She barely showered, look totally disheveled all the time, became even thinner and just stumbled around in her alcoholic haze. Her children would occasionally call her on the phone, even though it was far from pleasurable, listening to her booze-soaked ranting and raving. She pretty much burned every bridge due to her acid tongue, no one wanted to be around her.

On another hot and sticky afternoon, she decided to go lounge around on her float once again. She was already half in the bag but managed to arrange herself on top of the raft, the ever-present cocktail in tow. Of course, she didn't heed Angus' advice, and tether herself to the dock, so she aimlessly floated around in the tepid water. Being a weekday there were hardly any boats cruising the lake. She relaxed and dozed off, drifting here and there.

She lived four houses down from the dam and the recent torrential summer thunderstorm had raised the water level considerably. Water gushed quickly and dangerously over the spillway. The swift current drew her closer and closer to the swirling maelstrom.

Estelle was blissfully unaware of the perilous situation. Completely in her alcoholic haze, she had no time to react or scream as she was hurled over the edge of the waterfall. Her body went airborne as she left her raft and careened down the steep drop, smashing into the rocks below. It was all over. She lay in a crumpled heap, her body broken from massive internal damage.

Days later, her daughter tried to phone her, but got no answer. Over and over, message after message, all day and night. She knew her mother was prone to passing out after getting all sauced up, but she eventually snapped out of it. Her daughter had an ominous feeling.

She decided to go over. The door was locked, so she used her key.

"Mother! Are you here?" She looked from room to room — nothing. Also, no signs of any disturbance. She noticed the answering machine blinking, all those messages she left were not listened to.

She went outside to the patio and down to the lake. Nobody.

"Mom?" she called again. *No one takes a boat ride all day and hardly anyone likes her,* so she doubted that was the case.

She called her mother's estranged husband.

"Hello?"

"Hey Luke, this is Sophia — um — you haven't seen my mother lately, have you?"

He laughed shortly. "No, not for days. Not since I got out of that hellhole." He paused. "Are you at the house?"

"Yes. And I've been calling all day. There's no sign of her."

He sighed. "Well, I'm sure she's passed out somewhere. I'm sure she'll turn up soon."

"Yep, I'm sure."

"I think I'll stay out of this one. I'm sorry, Sophia."

"That's OK. I don't blame you. Thanks, bye."

"Bye."

She called the police, but they couldn't really do anything, a grown woman has a right to disappear without telling anyone, and there were no signs of foul play, but they would be on the lookout for a woman wandering around.

A week went by and still there was no signs of Estelle.

So, the cops came on scene and dispatched a forensics team to her house. But, they found nothing suspicious, no blood spatter, no unusual footprints, nothing at all.

They were informed about her drinking problem.

"Perhaps she had a few too many and somehow drowned in the lake," an officer speculated to Sophia. "We will have to see if the body floats up." He glanced at Sophia's stricken face. "Sorry to sound so morbid, ma'am."

She sniffled. "I know."

"You say she and her husband were estranged?"

"Yes."

"Not divorced yet?"

"No. He just recently moved out."

"I see." He jotted some notes down. "OK, we'll explore some other avenues. Thank you."

They paid a visit to Luke at his brother's house.

"I haven't seen her since I walked out on her." He ran a hand through his hair. "Living with a drunk is tough. Everyone has a breaking point."

"Rumor has it, you are having an affair?"

His eyebrows went together. "Oh?"

"And we know about the confrontation between your wife and your alleged mistress at the lake picnic."

Luke made an irritated face. "Do you know how many scenes Estelle has made? Just about every time she steps out in public. She's always bombed. I'm sure you know that, too."

"Yes, we do," the detective continued, "we know you got a little rough with her that day, as well."

Luke let out a sarcastic laugh. "Oh please — totally blown out of proportion by people who have nothing better to do than gossip and cause trouble," he scoffed. "I grabbed her arm and led her out of the party. She was, of course, hammered, and making a huge scene." He sighed heavily.

"Well, we have to look into everything. The spouse is always suspect number one."

Luke threw up his hands. "Look, I didn't kill her, harm her, or do anything to her! You want DNA, or you want a lie detector test, I'll do anything you want. I haven't touched that drunk for years. I'm not going down for this. This has been brewing for years — she's a careless, sloppy drunk, she did something to herself, I'm sure of it."

"Well, as of now there are no signs of foul play." The detective rose to leave. "We may be back."

"That's perfectly fine."

They went to see Heather Drake, as well.

"I don't know anything about that woman. Just that she's an obnoxious lush," Heather bluntly stated. "You should question half the people on this lake, she picks fights with everyone."

"So, we've heard. And what about you and her husband? The affair?"

She looked taken aback. "Affair?" She rolled her eyes. "I'm a masseuse. Everyone who gives massages has to be screwing their clients, right?" She disgustedly shook her head. "No affair. Boy, people just love to sully other people's reputations," she responded indignantly. "Rumor and hearsay rule the world. Pathetic!"

"We're just doing our job, ma'am."

"Oh, I know." She flung her arm out. "Please, look around. Go over the place with a fine-tooth comb. I have nothing to hide."

They searched around and found nothing.

"Thank you for your cooperation."

"No problem. I hope you find her," she called to them as they headed up the driveway.

"That woman causes more trouble — dead or alive," she whispered caustically to herself.

Luke and Heather were guests at another cookout on the lake. They ran into each other at the dessert table.

Of course, Estelle's disappearance was the talk of the party.

"I don't know if we should be seen chatting," Heather said in a hushed tone.

"Of course we can. I have nothing to hide, do you?"

"Not a thing."

"I didn't do anything to her, I'm sure somehow she did herself in." He shook his head.

A few heads turned in their direction.

Heather rolled her eyes. "The cops came to see me. Nothing was suspicious," she replied loud enough for the nosy people to hear.

They both turned towards the crowd.

"We didn't kill her, everyone," Heather irritatedly announced. "Find something else to gossip about. God knows on this lake there's plenty of material."

"See you later, Luke."

"Bye, Heather."

They went their separate ways.

A few days later, Sophia returned to her mother's house to see if she had missed something. Nothing in the house was missing, then she took a peek in the shed. It dawned on her that her mother's hot pink float was missing.

"She's in the lake," she told herself as her heart sank and she felt nauseous.

She called the police to inform them of her new information.

They dispatched a boat and a dive team. They didn't find anything. Then a few detectives went over to look around the dam, searching from the spillway to the stream that runs under a small bridge. Under the bridge, they found her, caught in some branches and debris. Her hot pink raft was further downstream.

Remembering Angus Macgregor's story of how she passed out in the middle of the lake and was almost killed by a boat, they presumed she did the same thing again, this time with fatal consequences.

No charges were filed. Just another tragic tale on Blue Lake.

Chapter 7

Come Kayak with Me!

Kathy Jones had left her lovely home in Naples, Florida after the accidental drowning death of her husband Vinny. She had sold their lovely home with its view of the golf course green and the lanai waters for just under a million dollars. It was worth at least $2.5 million but she felt the need to get away quickly as there were too many memories there. Anyway, she had collected on two insurance policies for her husband's death, one for $1 million, that she had taken out, and the other for $2 million which Vinny had bought himself from the urging of his friend Jim Butterworth, who had just joined a financial advice company. Vinny knew that Jim got a certain kickback from the policies he sold, so he went for the maximum life insurance policy to help his friend out. Upon Vinny's death, Kathy received a tidy lump sum and with the house sale, it added significantly to her nest egg.

Kathy was a real estate agent and made money hand over foot without really trying. The clientele of Naples was one of the wealthiest in all of Florida. She just had to show the client the house once and usually they bought it. She was exceptionally beautiful, and her blonde hair helped her in more ways than she could ever imagine. Her clients all wanted to be her neighbor and become a part of her social network. She obliged most clients with one or two evenings out after a sale, but quickly got bored by their neediness and terminated all contact abruptly.

In Naples, Kathy and Vinny had a fun-loving life. They had numerous friends who willingly testified at the police inquest after Vinny's death. Comments from everyone included 'what a happy marriage they had, how outgoing they were, how they loved fishing, camping, hunting, nature walks, bird watching, golf, and hiking,' the list went on and on. All extolled their exuberant and jolly lives within the community.

Vinny had disappeared the weekend before their 6th wedding anniversary. Everyone in the community shared their opinions about how sad it was especially as it happened so close to their anniversary. Kathy and Vinny had planned a big celebration at one of the night clubs downtown, with a list of 50 guests, which Kathy cancelled just the day before, as she had kept up her hopes for his reappearance.

Vinny had told Kathy on the early, wintery, Saturday morning of his disappearance.

"I'm going up to St. John's River to do some hunting today. Jim called me and said that now is the best time to go. All the ducks are wintering now. He took a trip up there last weekend and said it was spectacular."

It was true that the hydrilla weeds of the river provided the perfect place for the ducks wintering migration pattern.

"And," Vinny continued, "Jim said there's a blind that we could foray from. A guide can bring us there and show us the site. We will meet him in Sanford at the upper part of the river."

Kathy could tell Vinny was excited from the way his speech flowed so fast out of his mouth. She was slightly repulsed at this, although she did not show her emotions to him nor did she know why it repulsed her.

"It seems like you guys have everything sorted out then," she said. "How long will you be staying up there?"

"Oh, I'll be home in the evening, but it's going to be late, so don't stay up for me," he replied.

Jim and Vinny had a history of doing many outdoor activities together like hunting, fishing, sky diving and parasailing. This was quite fine by Kathy, as she used this time to entertain her present and previous clients. Jim and Vinny's male friendship was no threat to her happiness and she busied herself with her real estate work.

When she awoke the next morning, and Vinny had not returned, she tried his mobile. When she got no answer, she tried Jim's phone but also no luck.

"Jim what's going on? Where are you guys? Call me as soon as you get in!" She left a message on his phone, similar to the message she had left on Vinny's a few minutes previous.

Jim called back several hours later with the unwelcome news.

"Kathy, sit down. I have some troubling news for you. We didn't meet up with the guide yesterday. He was booked out for the day. I'm so sorry!" he wailed into the phone.

Kathy waited for him to continue, she felt her breathing quicken and her heart began to pound in her chest.

"So, we headed out on our own. I thought I knew the way but … " He broke down and there was silence.

"I lost him, Kathy, I lost him in the swamp. I've been searching for him all night. I don't know how but he's gone and there's no trace of him. I was with the police all morning and they are searching the area. They think the alligators must have gotten him."

"Oh my God Jim, this is crazy! No! No!" She began weeping into the phone.

"Kathy, I have to go and talk to the police again. They will be calling you shortly. I just wanted you to hear it from me first. I'll call you back later." He ended the phone call.

Kathy sat still in the chair, paralyzed for some time, until the phone rang again. This time it was the police, a man who identified himself as Detective Haas.

"Mrs. Jones, we regret to inform you that an accident has occurred, and your husband is lost in the northern river area. We are speaking with a friend of his, Jim Butterworth, and are searching the area he was last seen in. Let me reassure you that we will continue to search for him until he is found. From what Mr. Butterworth says, your husband is an avid outdoorsman and I am fully confident that he will be found before nightfall. Is there anyone there with you?" the officer asked Kathy.

"No," she weakly replied.

"Well," he continued, "I advise you to call some family or friends to be with you during this time. I will call you promptly with any news. I will also be sending some officers to your house to gather some more information about your husband. Expect them later today. Just stay at home, try to be calm and wait for our call. Thank you and realize we will do everything in our power to find him. Our K9 search team will scour the area for the next 24 hours. I will be in touch."

"OK," she said. She hadn't the energy to say any more.

The next few days were a nightmare of police questions and dashed hopes of finding Vinny. Jim had returned and sought Kathy out, but she rejected his advances and condolences. The K9 team had found nothing except cottonmouth water moccasins snakes and alligators.

Kathy had finally called off their 6th year wedding anniversary party at the club. A small group of friends came to the house on the Saturday night and the mood was solemn. They all tried to comfort Kathy and Jim but after six or seven days of searching the swamp, the police had offered no hope or signs of finding Vinny and everyone sadly agreed, he was gone.

It took six months to officially declare Vinny's death accidental, due to drowning, even though his body was never found. Jim had work tirelessly with the police to get them to agree to the accidental death verdict. He had some clout with the detective assigned to the case, for that Kathy was grateful at least and so the insurance company paid up.

It was now a year since Vinny's disappearance. She had purchased the lakefront house in Massachusetts, which had all the modern conveniences of her house in Naples. Although she was missing her in-ground pool, the lakeside was beautiful. Oak and maple trees dotted the uplands surrounding the lake. Ruby-throated hummingbirds buzzed their feeders, the sun blazed in a truly blue sky, and no trace of humidity in the air, a true paradise.

She put on her bikini and felt a surge of relief at the change of scenery surrounding her new home and lay down on a lounge chair to sunbathe. She had left Jim and all her friends behind in Naples to start a new life. She took the Massachusetts real estate licensing exam and passed effortlessly and immediately got a job with a broker. *Life was good*, she thought.

A sudden voice called from the lakeside, and she sat upright slightly startled. It was from a party boat with a single solitary man.

"Hello there. Welcome to our neighborhood. Would you like to take a tour of the lake? We're pretty much a very friendly and tight knit community around here. My name is Tim Connolly, come on down and I'll show you around." He laughed out loud in a contagious matter and she smiled back at him.

"Why not?" she responded and grabbed her cover up and sauntered towards the boat.

He began by chatting in an offhand way but deftly covering many personal and somewhat private issues. By the time they were halfway around the lake she had already revealed that she was recently widowed from Florida.

"I'm a real estate agent and a real good one too. Do you know of any houses for sale on the lake?" Kathy had decided to try and get some information from Tim.

He proceeded to inform her about every house, its history, its owner's history, what and when each had sold for, when it was built, what problems the house had, what the neighbors were like and tons of other incidentals. Within an hour, she had learned much from Tim.

What she didn't know was that Tim normally stopped and picked up every single person he saw on the lake. But not this time, Tim had given her an exclusively private tour which Kathy had enjoyed immensely. It was then that she realized she missed a man in her life, as she raised her hand brushing the hair back from her face, her eyes taking in this male physique with forgotten desire.

Wonder if I still got it? She smiled mischievously at Tim.

"So," she began, "what's your story?"

"Well I'm happily married," he said, "and a proud father of two college age kids."

"I was once happily married too." She sighed and looked overcast.

Tim brightened up and laughed engagingly at her. "Don't worry! There's loads of fish in this lake. I expect you will do just fine here. What say you come over to our house tonight? Meet the wife? I'll get a little barbecue going, invite some people over, you can meet some eligible neighborhood bachelors, have a little fun, good food, a few cocktails? Think of it like a welcome party! What do you say?"

"Alright it sounds like fun. Should I bring anything?" she asked.

"No, just your beautiful blond self." She was smitten by his reply. "I will see you at 6 o'clock then."

"Should I come and pick you up?" he asked.

"No that's okay. I have a kayak. It will do me some good to get some exercise."

"You look fine to me," Tim said, "see you later!" Before he could maneuver the boat close to the sandy shore line at her house, she dove off into the water and reappeared and swam to shore. *Strikingly mermaid like*, Tim thought to himself. He smiled at her and waved goodbye.

Tim returned home to inform his wife, Judy, of his welcome party idea for the new blond, female neighbor in the contemporary house.

"You know that house down the end of the lake, modern contemporary with the cupola, well she lives there." Tim walked energetically around the house, cleaning as he went from room to room. He had already called a few of his single buddies to come over, and two other couples.

"I've invited seven people, us, and Kathy, that's 10. That should be enough of people, don't want to scare her off!" He had to be careful about this, especially with Judy.

Who cares? thought Judy to herself. *Another bimbo on the lake, and a blond one at that. What the heck was with her husband anyway? Why did he constantly have to pick up strays?*

He was a friendly guy and she loved him for that but ... There was that 'but' again, rearing its ugly head. She didn't know quite how she felt about living here anymore. The sight of her neighbors appalled her, and she tried not to acknowledge their existence. Her life revolved around her work, her two kids and Tim of course. Her psychiatrist recommended anti-psychotics which seemed to work fairly well. But sometimes she couldn't shake off that bi-polar feeling. However, Tim seemed to be in good form this evening, so she would make an effort at entertaining their guests. He would do the cooking of course. He always did during the summer barbecues. She would mix cocktails and serve appetizers.

It would be fine, she reassured herself. "That's great Tim! We'll have a good time and make what's her name welcome."

"Kathy, Kathy's her name!" Tim tried to reassure his wife with his broad smile as he proclaimed the new neighbors name.

At 6 o'clock, Kathy paddled her kayak to Tim's house, and pulled it up on to the sandy shoreline. Tim's laugh resonated and she looked up.

"Hey Kathy," he hollered, "come on up."

She sauntered up the steps, her blonde hair bouncing around her.

"This is my wife Judy," Tim said, "Judy, our new neighbor, Kathy."

"Welcome to the lake!" Judy attempted politeness. "Can I get you a cocktail?"

"A mimosa, please!" Kathy eyed up Judy while smiling pleasantly at her.

"Definitely, be right back." Judy hastened towards the bar for the new blond neighbor's mimosa.

I'd like to give her a fucking mimosa right upside the head, Judy thought, *maybe a few other things too*! She smiled devilishly to herself. *OK, OK, shake off those negative ideas. Did I take my medicine today?* She couldn't remember. *Well then, I can have a drink at least!* She promptly poured herself a drink too.

She returned to Tim and Kathy armed with two mimosas. Tim looked puzzled at her.

Why was she drinking? This could be a crazy night, he thought with a sense of foreboding.

"Cheers!" Judy said, clinking glasses with Kathy.

"Thanks!" Kathy looked from Tim to Judy and back to Tim again. *Something wasn't right,* she thought but she chose to say nothing and just smiled.

The evening barbecue was a remarkable success. Kathy met two of the lake's eligible bachelors. One of which was quite to her taste, tall, blond and muscular, owned a few houses on the lake, some as rentals, and made his money also in real estate. They could certainly become a power couple on the lake, a force to be reckoned with in her mind. The other was a divorced man who had too much baggage, a sickly wife to whom he paid an unsightly amount of alimony, and three young children under the age of six, who demanded his continuous attention. He had shared all this with her in the space of five minutes. He wanted a mother for his children, and not a partner in life.

She immediately cast him adrift and focused her attention on getting more information on the tall, blond gentleman, Karl. The two other couples that Tim had invited were okay, a little stand offish though. The wives were tall, blonde and well-educated sisters. One owned a large horse farm down the road, and the other was a pediatric doctor. Their husbands had adequate good looks but were not as brainy as the two sisters. The doctor was married to an accountant who taught business at a local community college, and the horse farmer had married a veterinary doctor, now that seemed like a good match to Kathy.

The barbecue was going along extremely well. People were enjoying themselves and Kathy's presence, chatting amicably until things went awry. A female voice could be heard above the frivolous voices. It was Judy. She had obviously drunk more than one mimosa and was hurling insults at the two sisters.

"What's your fucking problem? You think you're so high and mighty the pair of you. I'll have you know I graduated top of my class. I'm better than the both of you put together." Judy gesticulated wildly at the two embarrassed sisters.

"You're very smart honey that's why I picked you to be my wife." Tim put his arm around her shoulder as he tried to soothe her.

"And what the fuck are you doing? Nothing! I make all the money in this house. I make twice your salary!" She turned her aggression on him.

This was close to true and offended Tim immensely. His face showed utter disappointment and dismay.

He looked towards Kathy and said, "I'm sorry about this but Judy isn't feeling well. I think it's time everybody went home."

Everybody was rather aghast at this drama but played along with it, wishing Judy and Tim a good night and thanking them for their hospitality.

Karl approached Kathy. "Can I give you a ride home?"

"No thanks" she said, "I'll just kayak home under the moonlight. Nice to meet you. Hope to see you again sometime."

"I'll be looking forward to that!" Karl beamed.

Kathy walked to the shoreline and pushed her kayak in and paddled off home. *Well that was interesting*, she thought. Everyone has their own story around here. It could be a good summer after all.

When Kathy got home, she reviewed the night's occurrences in her head repeatedly. *There's definitely something wrong with Judy, and poor Tim was at a loss. He needs to get rid of that wife, that's the only solution. But it's not my business really.*

The next day Kathy met Tim on the lake. He motioned for her to come to talk to him which she did obligingly.

"Want to go for a ride around the lake?" he asked.

"Sure," she replied.

Tim unburdened himself on their lake tour. He began, "Judy has a mental health issue. I didn't know that when I married her." He spoke of their love as a true romance but, as the years progressed, he noticed a dark side in her.

"I brought her to a psychiatrist and she was diagnosed with bipolar disorder," he explained. "There is a history of mental illness in her family, but the psychiatrist assured me that she would be fine as long as she took her meds." He sighed long and hard.

She obviously wasn't fine, thought Kathy, as she gazed deeply into Tim's eyes.

"Judy stops taking her medication whenever she feels good, just decides she doesn't need them. She is so difficult to control, especially if she has a drink." Tim stopped, at a loss for words.

"I can see that this is taking its toll on you," said Kathy, "don't you think you've done enough? Isn't it time for her family to step in?"

"Unfortunately, Judy's parents are both dead and she is an only child. She has no relatives to my knowledge." Tim looked dejectedly off into the distance.

"Maybe you can manage her medicines for her?"

"I've tried to do that," he said, "but she pretends to take them and, spits them out when I'm not looking."

"Maybe you should get a divorce?" Kathy broached the subject cautiously.

"I can't get divorced. I'm Catholic."

"Oh, I'm sorry. I'll see if I can talk to her. Help her in any way that I possibly can. I don't know anything about bipolar disorder, but I can try," said Kathy.

"Well that is very kind of you especially as you're new to the neighborhood, and we've only just met. I'd appreciate it though." Tim's laughter was nowhere to be seen or heard on their lake trip this time. He steered the boat back to Kathy's house and dropped her off.

"Thanks for the ride. I'll be seeing you around the lake." Kathy waved goodbye.

"Oh, by the way," Tim said, "what did you think of my friends, Karl and John?"

"Honestly John's got too much baggage, but that Karl is kind of interesting."

"That's good," Tim responded, "I knew you'd find a fish to your liking on this lake!" His laugh resonated briefly over the lake shoreline.

As she headed into the house, she realized she had to do something. *Tim was too nice a guy. Perhaps, he was the guy for her.* She mused to herself about this possibility. She would have to think about it.

Forget Karl, and have some fun with Tim. Perhaps build up some sort of friendship with Judy, try to talk some sense into her. Kathy quickly discarded that idea. *It was futile and a waste of time and energy.* She needed to come up with a strategy. *If she could get rid of Judy some way, Tim would be available.* She pondered this for a few hours and came up with a plan. She would invite Judy over for some tea to extend a hand of friendship. She went to bed satisfied with her scheme.

The next day, in the afternoon, she got the phone book of lake people which had been given to her. There was Tim and Judy's number and she dialed it. Judy answered.

"Hey this is Kathy, from last night. I was wondering if you wanted to come by for a cup of tea and we could hang out awhile and chat?"

Judy was a little perturbed as she realized she had made a bit of a scene at the party. She didn't remember anything, but Tim briefly mentioned her inappropriate remarks before heading off on his tour of the lake this morning. She resented his social life. *He goes around for hours picking up people on the lake, just like that new blond bimbo, Kathy from last night. And now here she is, in my fucking face, on the phone!*

"No thanks, I am a little busy," Judy lied.

"Come on, and take a break, you wanna go kayaking instead?" Kathy persisted.

"Well I really am very busy," Judy repeated.

"I heard that there's a beaver dam on this lake maybe you could show me where it is?" wheedled Kathy, and continued, "I don't have much time either really, just thought maybe half an hour or so. I will come to your house and we can paddle on from there. Isn't it only a little bit further down?"

Judy was beginning to ease up her negative stance.

"OK let's do it. But not too long," she said.

"Great! I'll be over soon!" Kathy hung up the phone and quickly readied her kit for the trip.

She carefully packed some cocktails into a small cooler and headed to the dock and up to the house in the kayak, scanning the waterfront for Judy. She was there and ready.

"Hey there girl! Let's go!" She greeted Judy like an old friend. Judy barely acknowledged her and descended into her kayak.

They paddled toward the end of the lake to where it began to narrow. The trees and brush were dense in these parts of the lake. The 2 kayaks eased their way upstream though winding small tributaries. Judy led the way.

"Watch this branch!" Judy held onto a low-lying branch and let it go abruptly at that instant.

A slight scream came from Kathy as the branch smacked her right in the face.

"You alright Kathy?"

Bitch! thought Kathy furthering her resolve to help Tim. "Yeah, it was nothing really."

After paddling for what seemed like ages, they began to hear the sound of a waterfall ahead.

"It's just around this bend," said Judy.

The weeds were dense here and the kayaks seem to glide just an inch above what could be land and then, there it was.

"That's amazing!" Kathy was truly impressed.

They eyed the dam looking for signs of beaver activity.

"It's a mini waterfall. Thanks so much for bringing me here. Hey, let's celebrate!" Kathy pulled out her mini cooler of cocktails.

"No thanks I'm not drinking," said Judy, "especially after the show I made of myself last night."

"I figured that, so I made one just for you that's non-alcoholic," Kathy answered.

"In that case, sure why not!" Judy said.

Kathy had the two containers ready.

"This blue one's for you and the red one's mine, danger, danger!" She cackled. "It's got the alcohol."

Judy took the offered blue container and slugged thirstily.

"My, that's salty!" Judy smacked her lips.

"Yes, it's a nonalcoholic margarita. I added extra salt as I couldn't coat the rim." Kathy smiled and laughed at Judy as she quickly drank half of her own cocktail. "Bottoms up!"

"Wow, you sure like to drink," said Judy. She glanced at the beaver dam again, as she took another lengthy swig and looked back to Kathy.

"So, what's going on with you and Tim?" Kathy probed Judy.

"What do you mean?" Judy was suspicious of her.

"I don't know, but at the BBQ last night you seemed to be coming down on him a bit hard and those two sisters? Don't you think, Judy?"

Judy looked at Kathy, focusing was difficult. "It's really none your business, stay out of it. Tim and I have been married a long time and we don't need no snowbird interfering!" Judy was angry, but the words came slowly from her mouth.

"Are you alright Judy? You seem to be a little agitated. Relax and this will go a lot quicker. Hand me that container of yours." Kathy reached over and grabbed the container easily from her hands.

"I don't feel so well," Judy said.

"Like I said, relax and this will go a lot quicker. Just listen to me," Kathy said, "you've been a bit of a bitch to that husband of yours, and so it's time."

"Time for what? Please help me!" Judy begged her.

"You're just a little confused." Kathy looked at her in disgust.

"I can't feel my legs anymore. We have to go back now." Judy tried to grab the oar to turn the kayak around and paddle home. But the paralysis had spread from her legs, up into her spine and arms. She suddenly felt a sharp pain in her chest area and gasped her last breath while her eyes rolled back in her head. After a few muscle spasms, she slumped forward.

"Well that was easy, bye-bye Judy!" She spoke to no one other than the beavers and birds.

Kathy sidled her kayak up to Judy's prone body, grabbed her arm and felt for a pulse at the wrist, nothing. She smiled again, packed away the cooler, and began to maneuver her kayak around slowly away from the dam. As she paddled, she admired her surroundings.

Yes, it was going to be fun living on this lake.

When she got to within earshot of any houses Kathy began screaming.

"Help, help, my friend is sick. She's at the beaver dam."

Kathy was looking up, anxiously scanning for someone to come out of their lake houses. A young couple were sitting on their deck and heard her screaming.

"What's going on?" an attractive male yelled to her.

"It's my friend, she's at the beaver dam. I came for help. I think we should call an ambulance. She's still there, she couldn't paddle, please help, call 911!" The words cascaded from Kathy's mouth.

"OK, OK, come on up here and we'll call," said the man.

Kathy raced up to their house. He dialed 911 and handed Kathy the phone.

"Please, please come quick, my friend, Judy, is sick! We were out kayaking and she's still at the beaver dam, I don't know what happened to her, but she couldn't move. We need an ambulance!"

"Where are you?" an authoritative voice asked her.

"I don't know, I don't know. Hold on." Kathy passed the phone back to the man. "They want to know the address." She began to cry. She knew how to put on a show.

The man took the phone from Kathy and gave the police his address and hung up the phone.

"They are coming right away." He guided the distraught Kathy to a chair and commanded, "Sit down and tell me what happened. I'm Pete Sampson and this is my wife Sharon."

And so, Kathy through sobs, relayed the story of their pleasant kayaking trip, and the unpleasantries that ensued.

"Okay, you stay here with Sharon and wait for the ambulance and I'm going to see if I can find her," Pete said.

He went down to the shoreline, grabbed a rope, got into the kayak and paddled quickly into the cove in search of the sick woman. When he got to the beaver dam, he saw the woman's slight figure hunched over in the kayak. It had drifted into the brush and there was no movement. Pete was anxious as he cautiously paddled up to the kayak.

"Hello, do you need help?" he said.

But the question was redundant as he quickly realized. She was dead. Pete was in shock. His hands were shaking as he knotted the rope to the dead woman's kayak. He began to paddle back to the house and heard the sirens in the distance approaching his house. As he got to the large opening of the lake, he could see in the distance, figures on the shoreline. They began running along the shore to reach him. He paddled with more speed towards them although he knew it was hopeless.

The two paramedics rushed to the kayak and pulled Judy's limp body out. They placed her on the ground, and one immediately began CPR. The other raced to the ambulance for the defibrillator and some Narcan, as they assumed an opioid overdose. After trying many times to revive the woman with the defibrillator and the Narcan, they stopped, covered her body and placed her on a stretcher, and carried her to the ambulance.

"I'm deeply sorry, but she's gone. Are you her next of kin?" one of the paramedics asked Pete.

"No," he replied, "she's a friend of this lady." He introduced Kathy.

At this point two police cars appeared sirens blazing. The paramedics and police communicated for some time, gathering the necessary information and then a policeman approached Kathy.

"I'm sorry about this and I understand you're upset about your friend, but can you give us some information please? What is her name? And describe what happened please."

Kathy relayed all the information about Judy to the police but neglected to tell them about her special cocktail and gave them Tim's phone number.

"Right, Miss, we'll take you home now so you can rest," said the police officer.

"I'd rather stay here awhile if you don't mind. I live right over there." Kathy pointed at her house.

"Sure," chimed in Pete and Sharon, "we'll see her home officer."

"We may need to talk again to you tomorrow about the incident. We will be in contact." The officer motioned for the paramedics and other officers to leave.

"Can I use your bathroom please?" Kathy asked Sharon.

"Sure, I'll show you." Sharon promptly got up and led Kathy inside her house to the bathroom.

"We'll be outside on the deck when you're done," said Sharon.

"Thanks for everything." Kathy closed the bathroom door and looked around. She relieved herself while taking stock of the lake house bathroom interior.

Wow there's a lot of boobs in here, thought Kathy and smiled like she hadn't a care in the world. *I'm going to like this lake living after all.*

Chapter 8

Still in Saigon

And then there's Frank Hudson, the mercurial divorced Vietnam vet, a perfectionist, who moved away for many years, much to the delight of his neighbors, who were practically dancing in the street. Unfortunately, he moved back after renovating the house.

He's the textbook bitter old man, with nothing better to do than cut his lawn, practically every other day, blast the leaf blower early in the morning and sit on his porch giving people the death stare if they dared to put a foot on his precious grass. God help the dogs who decide to poop on his lawn.

He routinely calls the cops on his long-suffering neighbors, or the Board of Health for anything he thinks is a violation. Everyone is sick of him. There is even speculation that he kidnapped the neighbor's beautiful Burmese cat.

But the neighbors are wary of him, leaving him alone lest they get a shotgun up the ass.

Being a perfectionist, he hires a maid service to come in once a week to completely clean his house. He is such a pain in the ass, many of them refused to come back. So, a new maid was to arrive today.

There was a knock on the door. Frank opened it to find a beautiful, petite Asian woman.

His eyes widened, and his head went back as he had a flashback to Vietnam, and the gorgeous Vietnamese that he fell in love with, and who broke his heart.

"Mai Ling," he greeted the woman, his voice trembling and low.

The woman furrowed her brow. "No, Sir, I am Li Quan Chu."

He looked confused. *She's changed her name*, he thought.

"Good to see you." His eyes devoured her. "Come in." He smiled brightly.

She was a little hesitant and uneasy, but she entered the house.

He couldn't stop staring at her. "How long have you been in this country?"

She thought that was a rather odd question right off the bat. *What is he, immigration?* she wondered. "I was born here, Sir, my parents came over a long time ago."

"Ah, I see." He grinned at her. "Please don't call me Sir. It's Frank, you know that."

He is a bit odd, she thought. She faked a smile. "So, Mr. Frank, where would you like me to start?"

He looked puzzled. "Start?"

"Cleaning."

"Oh yes, um — would you like a cup of tea first?"

"I would like to get my job done, please."

He was transfixed on her.

"Alright. The wash please, then a thorough vacuuming. The machine is downstairs."

"Thank you, Frank." She stepped around him and headed down the stairs, happy to get away.

"Another strange client," she said to herself, rolling her eyes.

He continued to watch her as she moved about the house, doing her job.

When she was done, she decided to herself that she wouldn't come back. There was an unpleasant vibe about him.

"I am done, Sir — Frank," she apprehensively informed him.

"Thank you so much." He held out some cash — $200.

Her eyes widened in surprise. "No Sir — too much," she politely protested.

"Take it, please. I'm sure you need it."

She smiled genuinely this time. "Thank you." She put the money in her pocket and headed towards the door. "Must get to next job."

He frowned. "Of course. But next week, same time?"

She hesitated a moment. "Very good, I will be here." She opened the door. "Goodbye."

He stared some more. "Can't wait."

As she sat in her car to drive away, she weighed the pros and cons of coming back, bizarre man, great money. She decided that she could put up with a lecherous old man for that kind of cash. She smiled to herself and drove away.

It was a decision she would soon come to regret.

A week later, she came back, right on time.

He was delighted. "Nice to see you, Mai – uh – Li Quan."

She felt a knot in her stomach, but entered the house anyway.

"Thank you ... Frank." She smiled tightly.

She puttered around the house, cleaning from room to room, aware of his hot eyes on her.

"Could you do a wash again, please?" he nicely requested.

"Of course." She went down the stairs.

As she was downstairs, he rifled through her purse, finding out whatever he could. He found her license, taking note of her address.

"Nice."

He found out which gym she goes to, and what bank she uses. He neatly put everything back into place, grabbed a beer and took a seat on the couch, a devilish gleam in his eye.

She returned upstairs and finished off the chores. She felt a little more relaxed, as Frank wasn't ogling her anymore, just watching television.

Good, she thought.

"I am all through," she informed him, heading for the door.

He rose and got the money to pay her — $200 again.

She took the money. "Thank you so much — you very nice man." She politely smiled.

He had the odd look on his face again. "So nice to see you again, my sweet."

She hastily backed away and headed out. "Bye."

"Until we meet again ... " he replied softly.

She wondered if she would return.

Following that day, Frank started doing recon missions on her, finding her apartment, noting her comings and goings, when she went to the gym, shopping etc.

After another creepy encounter with Frank, Li decided that she wouldn't go back to his house.

Frank was anxiously awaiting her arrival, it was the highlight of his week, seeing his Mai Ling again. When she didn't show up his fragile mind snapped. He flew into a rage.

"You won't get away from me again, Mai," he toxically whispered to himself.

One evening, around 8:30, Li got into her car and headed off to the gym. She was riding down the road when suddenly there was a movement in the back seat and a shadowy figure appeared. She screamed as a blade was brought to her throat in the blink of an eye.

"Don't do anything stupid, don't beep the horn, just drive where I tell you or I will cut you from ear to ear," a harsh, chilling voice warned.

She struggled to make out who it was in the dark. As she drove under a street light, she glanced in the rearview mirror and could recognize a face as the light briefly flashed.

"Mr. Frank what are you doing?" she pleaded, her voice frantic.

"You aren't getting away from me again, Mai," he viciously told her.

"I am not Mai, I am Li. Please don't do this. I don't know you!"

He put the blade closer to her skin. "Shut up! You lying bitch! You said you loved me!"

Li knew he was having a psychotic breakdown, so she had to play the game to try to stay alive.

"I'm so sorry, Frank, please forgive me. I will make it up to you," she begged, her voice soft. "Please, let's go somewhere and talk. You don't want to hurt me ... I ... I know you love me too much to do that."

He pulled the blade slightly away from her skin. "I do love you," he said tenderly.

She thought she might be getting to him. "Let's go to a restaurant and talk. Just enjoy each other again. I did miss you." She played the part well.

His tone softened. "Did you?"

"Of course, my darling."

He smiled and took the blade away. "Let's go to my house. You can fix me that special noodle dish that you used to."

She didn't want to be alone with him, for obvious reasons. Her mind was working like mad.

"I would love to. Let's stop at the store for that special sauce." She figured she could get away, cause a scene in the store if she had to — whatever it took to escape from this madman.

He laughed. "I forgot about that."

I may get out of this, she thought hopefully. "I can't wait to make you happy again," she said sweetly, wanting to vomit.

As they headed for the market, her phone rang. She cringed. *No!*

He peeked over her shoulder to glance at the mobile resting on the passenger seat. He read the name 'Mark.'

In an instant his demeanor shifted back to demonic. He put the knife back to her tender flesh. "You slut! I should slash you now!"

She inhaled sharply. "No, Frank, please don't do this!" she begged, her voice tinged with hysteria. "He's my workout partner — he's ... he's just wondering where I am."

"Enough lying!" he barked. "I'm so sick of the bullshit!" He let out a crazy wail that chilled her to the bone.

"That's it! You drive where I tell you to!"

Her stomach churned. She did as she was told, her hands shaking as she tried to tightly grasp the wheel.

They drove for a while, until they reached a lonely dirt road.

"Turn here," he bit out.

I'm not going to make it, she thought, screaming inside.

"Let's go to your house, baby."

"Enough!" he cruelly said in her ear as he roughly grabbed her hair. "Keep going."

She continued, then she saw his car parked in the distance.

What a psycho. What does he have planned? Her blood ran cold.

"Pull up next to my car."

She did as she was told, stopped her car, and peered out the windshield. The lights appeared to reveal a steep drop ahead, like the edge of a cliff.

She was sweating, her heart thrumming in her chest. *What the hell is he going to do?*

"Shut it off," he cruelly demanded.

She killed the engine and made one more plea for her life. "Frank! My God, please don't –"

Her cries were cut off by a cloth to her mouth, full of chloroform. She gasped and inhaled, then lost consciousness and crumpled forward.

Frank got her out of the car and placed her in his trunk. He then put her car in neutral, gave it a push, and watched it roll off the edge of the precipice.

As it turns out, this desolate place was an abandoned quarry where he frequently hung out as a kid. Very remote, the perfect place to get rid of practically anything.

He then nonchalantly drove back to his place, entered the garage and took her inside.

She groggily awoke, not sure where she was. Everything was quite hazy. She was in some unknown bedroom, lying on a bed. She had a headache and felt sick.

She rubbed her forehead. *Where am I?* She went to move off the bed, her head started spinning. It was eerily quiet. She tried easing off the bed again — then she noticed a cuff on her ankle — with a chain attached.

Dread shot through her body like a bolt of lightning. She started to hyperventilate.

Frank! she thought. *He did this.*

The events of the evening started to flash through her mind. *No!* She raced to the closed door. It was locked. She broke out in a cold sweat. "No! No! No!" She futilely hammered on the door.

Frank was conveniently keeping Li in a downstairs apartment, fully separate from his upstairs living quarters.

He had let his son live there for a while, but when he almost burned the house down leaving chicken cooking in the oven too long, he got booted the hell out. Frank now keeps it empty.

Being a security camera freak, he has lenses all over his property, watching every nook and cranny. He even has one in the downstairs bedroom, so he watched as Li awoke and went to the door.

Li was sitting on the bed, quietly sobbing, as the door handle movement caught her eye. Her eyes widened in sheer terror as Frank burst in, with a menacing smirk on his face.

"How are you, my sleeping beauty?" he cruelly harassed her.

She was still whimpering. "Why, Frank? Why?"

His cold eyes bored into her. "This was meant to be, you came back into my life. You are not going to be with another man."

He sat on the bed next to her and stroked her soft cheek as she stiffened her body.

"My beautiful Mai." He continued to be entranced by her, then finally broke out of his reverie and spoke again. "Come now, for your first night here I have made you something special."

He led her to the kitchen. Her tether allowed her access to a windowless bathroom and the kitchen, but it was short enough to keep her away from windows and doors.

This devil planned it all out. She shuddered. She had no appetite, the soup he made for her tasted like ash, but she choked it down to try to keep him on an even keel.

She also tried to prolong the meal as long as possible as she knew what was coming next.

It was after midnight, she had endured his drinking and psychotic ramblings about their past in Vietnam for hours now. She was so tired and distressed from the whole ordeal.

"Please Frank, I am exhausted, may I please go to bed?" she shakily asked.

His bloodshot eyes burned into her. "Ah, yes, it's time for the best part of our reunion." He kissed her cheek, he reeked of booze.

Li cringed. "Please Frank, I will make it up to you ... tomorrow," she pleaded.

He shook his head and got off the couch, a bit unsteadily.

"I've waited so long, my sweet." He grasped her hand and led her to the bedroom. "Let me show you how much I've missed you." He drunkenly laughed.

"Please Frank, you had too much to drink — go rest. We have the rest of our lives." She forced a tender smile.

He led her through the bedroom door. His grip tightened. His eyes got black.

"I will have you — Now!"

She couldn't help but let out a small scream as he sloppily forced himself on her. He cruelly clapped a hand over her mouth.

"Do that again and you'll regret it." His stale breath made her want to vomit.

After he finished, he rolled off her and went to sleep. She lay there, facing away from him, curled up in a ball, silently crying. The tears rolled down her face. She felt herself die inside.

This endless cycle of hell continued for days into weeks, as she became numb to the whole wretched scenario. She cooked his favorite meals, listened to him 'reminisce' about their time in Vietnam together, and satisfied his ugly needs. She basically lost the will to live, knowing she would never escape, but something kept her going. The kidnapped Burmese cat would visit her, and she clung to him, the only bright spot in this agonizing ordeal.

One evening, as Frank was relaxing and drinking on the couch upstairs, his doorbell rang. He was instantly on alert and dashed to his surveillance video feed.

Standing at the door was a young Asian man, holding a bag.
Frank's eyes became icy slits and his mind went off the rails.

"How the hell do they know she's here?" he raged. He went
to the door.

"Yes?" he called from behind the closed door.

"Chinese food," the man replied.

Bullshit! Frank told himself. *It's a trap. I didn't order any
goddamned food.*

He calmly opened the door and genially let the man in.
"Come in." Frank gestured towards the kitchen. "Put the bag on
the counter while I get the money." He cordially smiled.

As soon as the man turned his back on him, Frank shifted
into military mode and flashed back to Vietnam. With swift,
tactical precision, Frank came up behind the poor, innocent
man, put him in a hold, and instantly snapped his neck. The man
crumpled to the floor in a lifeless heap.

"No one is taking Mai from me, you shithead." He chuckled
sickeningly as he looked at the body.

By going to the wrong address, the unfortunate man paid
with his life.

Now to dispose of the car and the corpse.

Luck was with ol' Frank that night, as this was the evening of
a neighbor's annual blowout bash. On an adjacent street to the
lake, the Carson's were hosting their extravaganza. They were an
older couple, in their 50s. He used to be in a band, and just for
kicks and nostalgia, they still do a few small gigs a year. And
every year, the band gets back together for one night in the
summer at his house, partying it up in his barn. The band blasts
their live performance and the crowd gets boisterous. Cars cram
the driveway, front yard and park up and down the street.

Simply enough, Frank drove up the road and parked the
delivery guy's car behind the last car parked on the street — and
slipped away unseen into the darkness, after wiping down the car
for his prints. As they say the night time is the devil's
playground.

Now for the corpse. Frank wrapped the body in a carpet, taped it up and maneuvered it to the trunk of his car in the closed garage.

He drove not too far away to a part of the road that curved along a steep drop off, a stand of pine trees dotted the landscape.

Being out in the boonies, the road was desolate and dark, and it was after one in the morning.

Quickly, Frank doused his lights, ran to the trunk, and unceremoniously tossed the carpeted body off the edge of the steep hill. It rolled to the edge of the lake. He furtively drove away back home, still in his delusional Vietnam paranoia mode.

As for poor Li, she continued to languish in Frank's house, as no one could figure out what happened to her — she and her car vanishing without a trace. Missing signs went up for the errant delivery boy after they discovered his car.

Did he wander off into the woods? Or hook up at the party and meet with foul play somehow? Myriad scenarios ran through the authorities' heads. No body had been discovered yet.

Occasionally, Li couldn't help but let out a scream, and once in a while a neighbor would hear it, but they figured it must have been the television set. They didn't want to interface with Frank the looney toon, anyway. Alas, her screams were futile.

Desperation was taking over, and Li thought about killing herself for the umpteenth time, but her willpower allowed her to live and rise above.

One hot afternoon, she could smell the neighbor's steak on the grill wafting through the air and a murmur of conversation and laughter.

They must be having a party, she thought.

She knew their deck where they grilled was visible from Frank's house. And she also knew Frank was in the shower after mowing his lawn, she could hear water running. She was risking death, but had to try something at this point. She frantically searched the apartment for something heavy enough to hurl through the sliding glass door so that the neighbors should take notice. She was racing against time.

Nothing seemed sturdy enough, until she searched the oven drawer and found a cast iron skillet.

This has to do it, she prayed to herself.

Summoning the strength of Hercules himself, with all her might she tossed skillet through the air like a frisbee. It crashed through the glass with a loud shattering noise. She began screaming. "Help me! Please!"

Lo and behold, the neighbors heard the commotion and saw a skillet sail through the glass, while a woman screamed bloody murder.

"What the hell?" one said, bewildered.

"Holy shit, we better call the cops," another guy replied, whipping out his phone.

After reporting the domestic disturbance, the man wanted to go help the woman, but the owner of the house warned him not to.

"He's completely demented, off his rocker — you might get shot," he informed him bluntly. "Let the police handle it."

As much as it pained the man not to try to help that lady, he stayed in the neighbor's yard.

But they did yell to the woman that they had called for help as they peeked through the arborvitae.

Li fortunately heard the guy informing her that they called the police. All she could do now was wait and pray that they came before Frank killed her. She sat on the couch, shaking like a leaf, hoping that soon this would miraculously be over, and she would live.

After showering, Frank came downstairs, she could hear his footsteps coming towards her.

Bile rose in her throat and she prepared herself for the worst.

The pounding din of the shower water masked the frying pan crashing through the door, but now Frank glanced over and saw the hole and broken shards of glass.

He advanced on Li, with a murderous gleam in his eye. "What the hell have you done?" he viciously asked, his tone low and menacing.

This is it, Li thought, *the end.* She had to think fast. "The Vietcong are coming for you, you bastard. you are finished." She used his Vietnam hallucinations against him.

At the mention of the Vietcong, his eyes became wild and his face twisted up in rage, his mind instantly flipping back to the horrors of Vietnam.

"I will kill every one of those fuckers," he vowed as he turned and headed back upstairs.

Li couldn't believe her luck. Maybe she would make it, after all. She anxiously waited downstairs, wondering what would happen next.

Upstairs, several police cars swarmed the driveway. Guns drawn, a few cops headed towards the house.

Frank watched the action unfold on surveillance cameras. He was in full flashback hysteria mode.

"Let's do this," he whispered maniacally.

As the police descended on the front door, Frank came from behind his house, dressed in full army fatigues. He came barreling out, screaming like a banshee at the top of his lungs, an automatic rifle in his hands.

"You're all gonna die, you fucking gooks!" Bullets sprayed everywhere.

In an instant, the police turn towards him and open fire.

Gunshots crackled in the air as Frank was riddled with bullets. He staggered backwards and fell to the ground.

It was all over.

Li could hear the commotion. She had a knot in her stomach. She was rocking back and forth on the couch, crying, about to lose her mind from the intense stress.

Suddenly, a policeman came through the door. She burst into tears.

He noticed the woman was chained. A shocked look crossed his face.

"Please help me!" she wailed. Her face was a blotchy tear-stained mess, her eyes sunken and lifeless.

The man came towards her. "It's OK now, you're safe, the man is dead," he soothed and tenderly grasped her hand.

She burst into wracking sobs and hugged the cop. She was finally free.

A crowd of neighbors were gathered around, watching in disbelief. Suddenly, a cat sprang out of the open front door.

"Ginger! Oh my God!" A delightedly surprised voice rang out, "You were in there!"

The cat bolted towards his happy owner.

"That piece of shit did kidnap you! I knew it!" The woman hugged her pet and headed home.

So that was the pitiful end of Frank. No one could really say they would miss him, as peace and quiet would be restored in the neighborhood. Still, it was a tragic, unnecessary end.

Chapter 9

Catch of the Day

The two fishermen were on the lake just after sun rise. They usually anchored right outside Louloo's house and fished for hours. Two men, or was it a woman and a man, Louloo couldn't tell really. They were both dressed in checkered shirts and khakis with safari style large brimmed hats and sunglasses. Louloo was amazed at how they just sat there every day in their small motorboat, casting and reeling in, casting and reeling in. Funny, she never saw them get excited about catching anything. If she ever caught a fish, she would be hooting and hollering. But there was none of that, no hooting or hollering, or any celebratory laughter. Sometimes it looked as if they spoke to each other, as they nodded their heads, but you couldn't hear anything that they were saying. Normally, sounds carried all over the lake. One could practically hear a pin drop. But not these two fishermen, they appeared dedicated to their task of fishing. Louloo got bored watching them and pondered the merits of fishing.

What was the allure with fishing? "Ha, ha!" she chortled out loud.

"Allure and lure, I crack myself up sometimes," she said to her companion, a cute Westie dog, called Nessa.

It wasn't like they were going to eat the fish caught in the lake, although Louloo had herself eaten one, but the fishy taste of the huge, 25-inch largemouth bass repulsed her, and she swore, never again.

"If you can't eat it, there's no point in fishing. Right Nessa?" She lovingly rubbed the ears of her little Westie and promptly went about her usual chores of cleaning the large lake house.

The two fishermen sat in the anchored boat until one spoke.

"So how you feeling about today, Ron?" Kelsey asked of her fishing partner. "Do you think we'll get the big one today?"

Kelsey had just recently joined the FBI within the last year, straight out of college with a cybersecurity degree. She was enthusiastic about the work, but she wasn't too sure about this undercover operation.

Fishing day in and out, where's the action? she wondered. She had been doing this surveillance assignment for weeks and was not terribly enthused about it. She would have preferred to be where the other agent Jennie was, in the basement of the northern FBI house watching the dozen or so computer screens which monitored the surveillance cameras and listening devices. The team had set these up to catch a drug smuggler and break up his ring. But no, Kelsey was assigned to fish beside her much older partner, Ron. The bureau had decided that they needed to monitor lake access to the Santiago house, so they purchased a small cottage, at the southern end of the lake and installed Kelsey and Ron in it.

The two-person team reported daily of no unusual activity. The jokes from the other agents about how many fish they had caught, and when were they going to land the big one, dwindled as the assignment dragged on. They were after one big fish, Santiago, and he and his family were not biting, not yet.

"Well little lady, we'll just have to cast out and reel it in if it bites. Something is bound to happen today. I feel it in my waters," Ron answered her.

Kelsey shuddered with his response, *little lady*, she thought, *misogynistic prick! And what's his waters mean? Is that a reference to the bathroom?* She decided not to reply and just cast out again. Her earpiece spoke to her.

"Hi, Jennie here, just checking in. How's it going today, any action? Over."

Kelsey touched her earpiece and replied, "No quiet as usual, over."

"How's Ron? Over," Jennie asked.

"He feels something in his waters. Maybe it's the big one?" Kelsey sniggered at the thought. "Over."

"WTF? Over and out!" Kelsey's earpiece went quiet.

Kelsey and Jennie had developed a fast friendship uniting as modern females struggling in the patriarchy of the FBI. Times were changing but female leadership and mentoring were definitely lacking in the organization.

Kelsey's fishing partner, Ron, was a honed veteran of the agency. Ron had been previously assigned to undercover work on the cartels in Columbia, but since the arrest of 'The King Pin' he had been transferred to the east coast bureau to help.

Ron was thoroughly enjoying this assignment. He needed to unwind after the hectic times in Columbia. His female partner was a bit of a disappointment as she was a newbie and wanted to get into the darker parts of the FBI, a liberal feminist too, but he was happy. The Columbian cartels were crazy and one false move could find a person minus a limb, if you were lucky, or 6-foot underground if you were not. He had survived many a close call and this lake was just what he needed. He woke up excitedly every morning at the crack of dawn, showered and had some breakfast and then headed out on the lake to spend a good 6 to 8 hours fishing. It was always at the same spot, right outside Santiago's house but this was not deemed unusual or suspicious as fishermen tend to have their favorite fishing spots. His fishing partner, Kelsey had recently suggested that they just use the hooks with no bait or lures as she was fed up catching and releasing too many fish. The lake was swarming with large and small mouth bass and had recently been stocked with trout but he reluctantly agreed to her suggestion. They were to watch the house and report any activity back to their command post. So far, they really had nothing to report; a few fish were caught but not the big one.

"Did you hear that?" Kelsey asked.

"No, what?" Ron scratched his ear wondering if his age was beginning to affect his hearing.

"There's some people yelling, listen," Kelsey replied slightly irritated at the deaf, old guy beside her and she pointed the sound amplifier in the general direction of the dispute.

"Yep, I hear them now. It's a man and woman fighting, probably a domestic issue, same old crap." Ron pulled out his binoculars.

Kelsey struggled to pinpoint the source of the argument as the voices began to get louder.

"Look, over there!" She pointed to a house 5 doors up from the Santiago one. "It's coming from that house."

There was a car parked beside the house. Kelsey took out her binoculars to see if she could read the license plate. She recognized the Florida oranges on the plate and touched her earpiece and spoke into it.

"Jennie, I think we have an issue here. Can you trace this Florida plate for me? AG7 189, there's a disturbance 5 doors north of the target, over."

"Gotcha, will advise, over," said Jennie efficiently.

A man suddenly appeared from the house pulling a reluctant female with him. She struggled against him, as he pushed her into a chair on the deck.

"Are you getting this Ron?" Kelsey asked of her partner who nodded touching his earpiece too. The amplifier was now focused directly at the house of the disputing couple.

"What the fuck? What's your problem? I thought we agreed about what was going to happen after the accident." Ron heard the male's voice in his earpiece.

"Just a dispute of some sort, domestic bull shit," said Ron, "no worries little lady."

There was that little lady comment thing again, Kelsey bristled. She touched her earpiece and heard Jennie's voice.

"The house in question is inhabited by one female, Kathy Jones. She was recently involved in an accidental death on the lake of another female neighbor, Judy Wood, deemed heart attack, still checking the reg plate, over."

Ron had moved the boat closer to the house to get a better view of the goings on. The couple appeared to have quieted down and were sitting calmly on the lake side deck. Kelsey's earpiece came on.

"The car is registered to a Jim Butterworth from Florida. He was questioned about the accidental death of Vinny Jones, his friend is the female's deceased husband," Jennie stated.

"So ... they're friends," said Ron, "the dead husband's best friend comes visiting to cry on her shoulder?"

Kelsey had her suspicions raised too.

That was not the screams of a surprised women glad to see her husband's friend but one in danger, she thought.

"Chief relayed in, continue to monitor but don't interfere, as it may compromise the job," Jennie's voice came over Kelsey's earpiece.

As Kelsey and Ron continued to watch the couple talk, the male abruptly got up and then fell to one knee.

"Look, he's impersonating Kaepernick or else he's proposing," Ron said, "isn't that sweet?"

"No way! I'm not marrying you!" The female raised her voice and shrieked as her body language changed from complacent to agitated.

"You have to be my wife. Don't you get it? I don't want you testifying against me. You know that we both agreed that Vinny had to go. You agreed to it. You got all that money too! Don't fuck with me. You're in this as much as I am." The man paced back and forth on the deck.

"I never loved him and certainly not you for that matter. Let's try to get this straightened out. I wouldn't testify against you Jim, not in a million years. I realize that if it wasn't for you, I would still be in that shit relationship. Come on now and think this out. If you want some more money, I'll get it for you." The woman appealed to the man.

The two fishermen maintained their cover, casting and reeling in apparent disregard of the dispute unfolding before them.

Kelsey felt a surge in adrenaline; *this was more like it, a little action.* "What you think Ronbo?" Kelsey used the nickname of the veteran FBI agent. It was the first time she had called him by it.

"There's a slight discrepancy. Seems the lady doesn't want the ring," he casually replied.

"Maybe we should call it in. Her husband dies in an accident and now his friend is saying she was involved. You heard that stuff about money and testifying. It seems like something's fishy here." Kelsey smiled at her pun.

"You're losing focus. We're after the big fish not this minnow. No, this isn't what we're here for," Ron said simply.

"Oh come on. This is something at least. Let's head back to base. I'll take a run over there and see what's going on, be neighborly like. Ronbo, please!" Kelsey was dying for a little action and now smiled broadly at the veteran agent.

"Just for the record, I'm in disagreement with this, but I have to use the bathroom, so OK." Ron slowly steered the boat towards their base.

The voices from the deck grew loud again in disagreement. The fishermen watched as the male stood up and approached the sitting female.

"I have thought about this more than you know. I don't trust you. You will testify against me so the only way to solve this is to get married. So, come with me now. We're going to get hitched!" He held out his hand to the woman.

"You're gonna have to kill me first or should I say over my fucking dead body!" the woman screamed back at him.

With her retort, the man took full swing at the seated woman. The force of the blow sent her flying off the chair. She lay in stunned silence as she recovered from the blow.

"You mother fucker! If you think I'm marrying you, you're fucking nuts." She had barely got the words out of her mouth before the man grabbed her and dragged her across the deck to the stairs.

Louloo had heard the noise and screams coming from next door when she stopped vacuuming.

"Nessa what the heck is going on next door?" The dog was barking crazily. Louloo went outside and saw Kathy, her new neighbor, being dragged down the stairs by a man. She shouted at them, "I'm gonna call the cops right now, unless you stop! Leave her alone!"

The man looked over and saw her. He paused and then pulled out his gun and aimed it at her. "Shut up bitch, or I'll give you some of this."

Louloo screamed and ran back into her house, looking for her phone frantically. There was too much stuff going on in this neighborhood, and she was fed up of it. She dialed the police and reported the threatening man with the gun next door, locked all the doors and then went and hid the basement with her dog.

The fishermen were watching as the scene escalated. They saw the neighbor come out and the struggling couple heading down the stairs, the male waving what might have been a gun. Ron accelerated to the base as Kelsey heard from her earpiece.

"Local police called us, weapon drawn at your house. Investigate immediately. Kelsey you get that? Local PD are on their way, over."

"On our way, over and out Jennie," Kelsey said. The boat docked and she scrambled out running to her car and jumped into the driver's seat.

"Come on Ronbo! We gotta move it!" She leaned over and opened the door for him.

Ron jumped in and they headed towards the house. It was only a few minutes away. As they neared the turnoff for the lake road, they saw the Florida registered car accelerating towards them.

"That's him, but where's the woman?" Ron said.

"Should we go to the house or follow him?" Kelsey asked of her veteran partner.

"The local PD is heading there now, so they will deal with her. Let's go get us this Florida orange and squeeze him a little!"

Ron took out his favorite handgun from his boot, stroking it lovingly.

"Let's get him!" Kelsey replied as she expertly turned the car around accelerating in pursuit.

She caught a glimpse of the Florida car in the distance turning right and raced on to follow him. The roads were narrow, windy and hilly as they followed the lake topography. She thought they had lost him at an intersection at bottom of one of the hills. Then they heard a woman screaming in the distance and screeching tires.

Jim had enough of Kathy's refusal of his marriage proposal, especially after that nosey neighbor came out yelling about the police. But he scared her off by threatening to shoot her. *That's it!* he thought. He drew back and gun-slapped his future bride in the face, knocking her out. He slung her body over his shoulder and threw her in the back seat of the car and drove quickly away.

"Going to the chapel, and we're going to get married ... " he sang out as he drove the unfamiliar roads around the lake. "Honey, join me. Gee, I really love you and we're going to get married ... "

Kathy was coming around. Her face hurt, and she was in a heap in the back of a car. *This is a fucking nightmare*, she thought. She realized she had to act fast before Jim realized she was conscious. She sprang over the car seat and grabbed the wheel sending the car careering off the road.

"I told you, over my dead body!" she screamed.

The car careered down the slope bouncing off trees like a pin wheel until it flipped and she was thrown from the vehicle. When the car finally came to a stop, Jim gasped his last words. "I loved you Kathy, I did it all for you." A tear fell from his cheek.

"It came from up there!" Ron pointed to the right and behind them.

Kelsey did a U-turn and flew up the windy road past one bend and another and another, the tires screeching as the vehicle swept the hill. They stopped sharply at another intersection at the top of the hill and listened. There was a loud crash from behind them.

"Go back!" Ron said.

Kelsey expertly turned the car around.

"Just there, through the trees. Looks like he went off road!" Ron pointed to the bank.

They stopped, got out and looked down the hill. They drew their guns as they cautiously peered through the haze of smoke wafting upwards toward them.

Kelsey went first cautiously down the hill, with Ron slowly following. They did not get far until the car exploded and burst into flames. The two agents waited for a brief time and watched the car burn. Kelsey went closer to see if the driver was there and called it into Jennie.

"Suspect dead in car, send fire truck and ambulance." Kelsey put away her firearm. "It's over. He's a goner."

"Yeah, got what he deserved I expect." Ron looked at the car engulfed in flames and sighed. Car bombings were normal in Columbia and he thought of the many times he had avoided getting himself blown up by the cartel.

"Kelsey, over," Jennie's voice sounded in Kelsey's earpiece.

"Here over," Kelsey responded.

"Local PD at house says no sign of female resident, Kathy Jones, over."

"What? She's not in the car, Jennie, but will look around, over," Kelsey scratched her head and looked over at her partner. "Turns out we have a missing female. She definitely wasn't in the car, right?" Kelsey questioned her partner, "Maybe she was thrown out of the car or do you think she's in the trunk?"

"If she was in the trunk, she's dead now. If she survived getting thrown out of the car, she could be anywhere in these woods. Call for a K9 team. In the meantime, I'll have a look around. You go up and wait for the local first responders!"

Ron took charge of the novice agent. Kelsey was beginning to irritate him with her lack of insight, although her suspicions had been right about this guy. He'd have to give her that.

Kelsey reluctantly agreed to her partner's suggestions, although it seemed more like an order. She rationalized it would look like she was in charge if she met the others at the top of the hill. *And good old Rombo was no Rambo,* she thought, *he probably couldn't make it up the hill too easily,* and she smirked to herself.

Ron wandered around the woody area for a short time before he came across an old campfire and some empty beer bottles at the lake shore. *Someone had a fun time,* he thought, and kicked at the charred logs. He looked down the lake and could see the local PD's flashing lights on the other side. *This might blow the whole case,* he reluctantly admitted to himself. *Well it was good while it lasted,* he thought as he headed sadly and slowly up the hill.

As he surveyed the woody area, he caught sight of something unusual, a rolled-up carpet. His instincts were heightened as he approached the carpet. The smell was not right. It wafted up his nostrils. He was too familiar with this stench of human decay.

"Kelsey," he radioed his partner, "I found something, not our bride-to-be but another one. Get CSI to come out here ASAP. Postpone the canines till after CSI is here and gone, over."

"Another body? Sure, will do, over," Kelsey said. *This was getting better and better.* She smiled. She loved her job and now the lake was heating up and she was catching some fish. *So what if it wasn't the big fish, a deranged man and a dead body are definitely good resume builders!*

When the fire truck and ambulance got to the scene, Kelsey greeted them. "Car and suspect are down there." She pointed down the hill. "My partner is waiting for you. CSI have been called for another body, so be careful where you step."

The firemen and paramedics proceeded down the hill to examine the smoldering car and its occupant. When they were half way down the forested hillside, Kelsey heard some excited chatter and someone shouted up to her.

"We found your missing female, looks like she died on impact with this tree. She must have been thrown out of the car."

Kelsey smiled to herself. "And that makes three," she said to no one in particular.

Chapter 10

Never Trust A Pretty Face

The sun glistened off the candy apple red metallic paint of the $70,000 ski boat as it slowly cruised down the lake. The top of the line stereo system boomed, and heads turned to admire the sleek craft. It was a real beauty.

Its owner was Victor Santiago, who just bought one of the most expensive houses on the lake. Coincidently, his daughter has recently purchased a stunning home on the lake, as well.

Some people wonder how they came to be so wealthy, as they only run a small landscaping business ...

Some people are also curious as to why a seaplane makes routine landings on a small lake in the middle of nowhere ...

The aircraft buzzed in the air as it circled the lake once and then touched down.

"It's here," Victor announced to his daughter, Valentina.

The paddleboarder glided by his house again, and Victor couldn't help but openly gawk at her.

Tall, tan, and trim, with long, toned legs, tight ass and a flat, muscular stomach, she was hot as hell. Her thick, long brunette hair fell like a curtain of silk down her back. And she had a great rack.

Victor himself was incredibly attractive. He was single, after an acrimonious divorce, and quite the ladies' man. He had a lot going for him — houses, cars, power, wealth, everything that women look for. He figured he could definitely have a go at the athletic beauty that always goes by. He had to at least try. His body tightened and as he watched her muscular physique maneuver the oar. Next time he would make his move.

The lady in question, was Giovanna Toscana, a full-blooded Italian goddess! The whole package — looks, brains and personality. She caused a stir wherever she went — she could have any man she wanted.

Victor was nonchalantly sitting at the edge of his dock, at a wrought iron, little table for two, sipping a beer, the next time she came by.

"Looks like a great way to keep in shape," he called out, a roguish smile lit up his face.

She flashed her dazzling teeth. "It is. Works lots of muscles, good for your core."

He ran his eyes up and down her fabulous bod. His body responded once again. "It certainly does."

Got him! She laughed to herself.

He lifted a beer from the cooler at his feet. "How about some refreshment?" he offered smoothly. "Come sit and have a drink. No funny business, just right here out in the open."

She hesitated a moment. "Uh — OK." She smiled. "I could use a break." She paddled around his gleaming boat and headed for shore, then propped her board on the dock and headed towards him. His eyes never left her.

"I'm Victor." He gave her the beer.

"Giovanna."

"Beautiful name, you don't hear it too often."

She sipped her drink. "True. Very popular back in the old country."

"Ah." He nodded. "No doubt. So, do you live on the lake?" he continued, very interested.

"I'm renting a house for the summer." She scanned the lake and pointed to a small log cabin style house across the way. "That one."

He followed her hand. "Oh. Very nice. Looks cozy."

"It is. It's perfect for me. I don't need something large, as it's just me there," she volunteered.

Nice, he deliciously thought.

She actually found him handsome and engaging. They bantered back and forth and enjoyed themselves.

"That's one hell of a boat," she enthused, gazing at the magnificent vessel.

He grinned from ear to ear. "Thank you." He paused. "How about a ride?"

She looked a little dubious. "Um ... next time."

"Come on, I'm not drunk, if that's what you're worried about. I wouldn't put you in jeopardy," he said sincerely, "it's a perfect afternoon for it."

"Well, OK." She smiled flirtatiously. "I would love to!"

"Great!" He grabbed the cooler and headed for the boat, stepped in, then graciously assisted her. They amiably chatted while enjoying the warm sun and lovely surroundings.

"What do you say we open this baby up," he excitedly suggested, referring to the boat.

She giggled cutely. "Let's do it!"

"Awesome!" He pushed the lever, the motor roared to life and rocketed down at the lake, rock and roll thundered through the air.

She let out a thrilling whoop as her hair flew sexily in the wind. They laughed, thoroughly having fun. It was such a rush!

After powering around the lake, they returned to his place. They exited the boat and stood on the dock.

"Thank you so much for the ride," she enthused enchantingly as her brown eyes glowed.

"Anytime." He couldn't help but check her out again.

She turned to go.

"How about dinner sometime? The best restaurant around?" He smiled.

"Sounds great!"

He took out his phone and asked for her number.

"I can't tell you how much fun this was." She flipped her long hair seductively.

"Total blast." His body reacted to her again. He groaned to himself.

"I must go."

"Right, I will definitely be calling — soon."

She positioned herself on the paddle board. "Good. See you soon." She gave him one last groin-tightening smile as she paddled away.

"Holy shit, what a babe!" He frustratedly ran a hand through his hair and longingly sighed.

They had a wonderful dinner together, then more dinners, boat rides and drinks on the deck. She even got him to go paddle boarding with her. Pretty soon they were inseparable. They were the hottest couple on the lake.

One pleasant afternoon while they were on the deck enjoying a cocktail, the seaplane buzzed over the lake again. A strange look crossed Victor's face, but he quickly recovered, continuing to chat with Giovanna.

"That's an unusual sight, a plane like that out here, on this obscure little lake," Giovanna casually commented.

For a split second, Victor looked concerned. "Yes, I agree. It comes by fairly often. I think he has friends on the lake."

"How cool!"

"Indeed." Victor quickly downed the rest of his beer.

"Excuse me one moment. I need another drink." He got up from the chair. "Need anything?"

She was dipping a potato chip into some guacamole. "No, thank you." She popped it into her mouth.

He gave her a quick kiss. "Be right back, gorgeous."

She laughed.

He entered the house and disappeared from view.

Victor was in the bathroom making a phone call.

"Valentina, you need to take care of this one — I have a guest."

After the terse call, he grabbed some more beers and returned to his beautiful companion.

She sensed a change in his mood. "Something wrong?"

He had a faraway expression. "What? I'm fine. Good guacamole, huh?" He grinned.

"Delicious. I should stop eating it, but I can't."

"You have a rockin' bod," he complimented her, his eyes raking over her. "You can eat all of it — we can work it off in bed later," he said seductively.

She lightly blushed. "Mmm – OK."

They sat there a while longer. Victor kept a sharp eye on the boats going by.

"Let's go for a ride."

"Alright."

They cruised around. He seemed preoccupied, watching every boat come out of the cove. Then he spied his daughter and her boyfriend motoring out of the cove in their fishing boat. They were quite far away but his daughter waved and gave them a big smile.

"That's my daughter."

Giovanna cordially waved.

Victor seemed to visibly relax a bit more. "I wonder how the fishing is." He picked up speed and headed towards the pines. They neared Giovanna's house.

"Tell you what — go put on your sexiest dress and get all dolled up. I want to take you for a night on the town." He smiled charmingly.

"Ooh, sounds awesome. I love dressing up."

He pulled up to her dock.

She kissed him and got out. "See you soon, sweetie."

"Can't wait."

She watched him blast away. "Oh yeah, something fishy is going on here," she told herself.

The next time she was over at his place, after some vigorous afternoon love making, Victor hopped in the shower and she decided to do a little snooping.

She quickly dressed and headed for the garage. Knowing time was tight, she frantically opened some tool drawers, rifled through a few cabinets, and looked under some tarps. Nothing. Everything was above board.

She shrugged her shoulders and raced back to the bedroom. She was brushing her luxurious hair as the bathroom door swung open. She couldn't help but stare at him. He was clad in a towel that was wrapped around his waist. He had great broad shoulders and a chiseled chest.

Damn! He is fine!

He smiled at her as she checked him out. "What?" he teased.

"Just enjoying the view," she purred. She crossed the room and embraced him. "Now, before I tear off that towel and we go for round two ... I have to go home and freshen up for the party at the neighbors tonight."

He frowned. "I'd rather stay in bed."

She moaned seductively. "I know, but we should make an appearance."

"I suppose."

She rubbed his butt cheek. "Alright, I better go." She kissed him. "See you later."

They continued to have an idyllic summer together — socializing, great sex, and thoroughly enjoying all the lake had to offer.

The next time the seaplane thundered in the air, Giovanna happened to be at her place. She stepped on to her balcony and saw the plane flying low, coming from the cove. It then gained altitude and flew away. She took a seat and patiently waited.

After a little while she saw a fishing boat headed into the cove. She didn't have a great view of the cove, it was quite a distance, so she went in and grabbed her binoculars. She focused in on the occupants of the boat. Victor and his daughter.

How interesting, she mused to herself.

She observed them trolling into the cove, and after a short while, motor out.

She sadly shook her head. *I'll get to the bottom of this.*

The following day she made a point of going to visit Victor.

She deliberately enticed him into the sack.

After some intense sex, he took a shower, as he always does. She knew that and counted on it.

Giovanna once again went to poke around in the garage. This time, a pickup truck, with their landscaping company name emblazoned on the door, was parked inside. It was full of shrubs and bushes ready to be sold and planted, with burlap bags covering the root ball. It was also full of bags of lime.

Lime – white powder, she pondered to herself. Her eyebrows shot up. On a hunch she hastily unfastened a burlap sack on a tree and peeked in. Small packets of pills, in clear little baggies were inside.

A rush of emotions flooded her, from disgust to terror, to sadness. She zipped back upstairs.

He found her relaxing on the deck, sipping red wine.

She smiled at him. A despondent look flashed briefly over her face, then vanished as she composed herself.

"Come, darling," she beckoned, "join me."

Back at her place, her voice trembled as she made a phone call.

"This is agent Toscana. I have confirmation of drugs. Coke, heroin, pills, the whole nine yards," she informed her connection.

She nervously stroked her hair. "I'm pretty positive they come in via seaplane, get dropped in a swampy cove, no houses, very remote, only accessible by small watercraft. It's an ideal place, a perfect scenario ... "

After her call, she sank wearily onto her bed. She held her head in her hands and quietly sobbed.

She had a raging headache and felt queasy, all the stress kicking in. She was seriously toying with the idea of letting him get away with it. She was in love. She also immensely enjoyed the lavish lifestyle, being blissfully wined, dined and pampered.

She felt a tremendous sense of accomplishment. She got the job done, a real feather in her cap, most likely one of the biggest busts of her career.

Myriad of emotions once again coursed through her but she mostly felt miserable. She had to go deep this time and go deep she certainly did.

Being a consummate professional, she had to do what she had to do. She poured herself a stiff drink — double vodka, and prepared herself for a hellish day, busting Victor.

The next day was a Sunday, she went to spend one last afternoon with Victor. She peeked into the garage — the truck was still there, loaded and ready.

It must be heading out tomorrow morning to his business — or to wherever — for disbursement.

She blew out a long, weary breath, then headed to the bathroom to text her associates to move in.

They were on the deck, cuddling on a lounge chair, laughing and teasing each other like lovers do, just enjoying the moment. She gave him a long, sensuous, loving kiss — one last time. She snuggled on his chest. She had a wistful look on her face, which he couldn't see.

"This has been the best summer of my life," he said, stroking her silken hair.

"Mmm — mine too." She cringed inside.

Not long after, there was a knock on the door.

She felt her stomach drop.

"Maybe it's Valentina," he said.

She got off of him as he rose to get up.

He opened the door. Two well-dressed men stood there, flashing badges.

"DEA. We have a search warrant for this address. We have reason to believe there are drugs on the premises," one man sternly informed him.

"What the fuck is this?" Victor bellowed. "Total discriminatory harassment!"

Giovanna had come from the deck and was standing behind him. "There are drugs in the truck in the garage, secreted in the shrubs and lime. I saw them myself," she stated seriously, completely stone faced. "Go see for yourself."

Victor swung around to face her, his face red with rage and shock. He came face to face with the badge in her hand.

"Are you fucking serious?"

"Agent Toscana, DEA," she bluntly stated.

He lunged for her throat but was restrained by an agent.

"Venomous bitch! Goddammit, I knew this was too good to be true!" he snarled. His eyes took on a lethal glow. "Lying shrew!" He was practically apoplectic.

Giovanna stood there, playing the tough-as-nails — I don't give a shit persona to perfection, but inside she was broken and crumbling. "Shut the hell up, you are fucking done," she scoffed derisively.

"You are dead, bitch. I will kill you — or have you taken out," he warned in a low, chilling tone. "This was your last hurrah. This was a bad move, enjoy your last days alive."

She rolled her eyes. "Oh, please, you are so pathetic." She stoically maintained a brave face.

An agent returned from the garage. "We got him. Drugs are affirmative."

"Get him out of here," Giovanna hissed. She was dying inside.

An agent cuffed him and hauled him away.

Her eyes were bright — she was desperately holding back tears.

"Fuck you," he muttered." His eyes were shooting daggers at her.

They raided the landscaping business and found copious amounts of contraband. The 'Pablo Escobar' of the lake was finished.

Needing to decompress and take a relaxing break, Giovanna booked a long vacation to Italy.

Chapter 11

Your Cheating Heart

Elsewhere on the lake in a newly renovated Cape Cod style house we have Connie and Walter Weston, both late thirties. He is a long-haul trucker, and she is a clerk at a department store. They have three children. They married young, had children at a fairly rapid pace, and now all is not well.

With her husband gone most of the time, child rearing is all on her shoulders, year after year. The tedium and loneliness of her life has taken a toll. She's become terribly depressed and resentful of her husband. On top of that, the stress and long hours of her husband's job often leaves him moody and ornery. He sometimes gets physical with her.

The same old story — she's afraid to leave, can't afford it — and doesn't want to ruin her children's lives or have him become violent with them. So, she loads up on antidepressants and keeps herself busy by exercising, especially enjoying all the aquatic activities the lake has to offer.

She loves to swim, kayak, and use their paddle boat. She's kept herself in very good shape and still enjoys putting on a bikini and sunning herself in a lounge chair at the end of their dock.

She's made quite a few friends that way, people tend to be very friendly riding around in their boats, trolling by fishing, paddle boarding — even floating by on tubes and rafts.

Quite often she gets offered a ride and readily accepts, happy to socialize and escape her dull life.

One man in particular has caught her eye – he routinely motors by — sometimes alone and often with a boatload. He always says hello and exchanges a few pleasantries with her, with a captivating smile on his face.

She doesn't know his name, but she finds herself looking for him, the man in the sea foam green party boat. She makes sure to be all dolled up, with a great bikini on — and gets quite disappointed when she doesn't see him.

One sweltering July afternoon, when you are so grateful to live on a lake and be able to dip in and out and feel totally refreshed, she was once again sunbathing in her favorite spot. Wearing her sexiest black bikini, all oiled up and quite tan already, she looked pretty amazing. She was lying there, on her back, eyes closed, languishing in the sun.

A whistle jarred her out of her day dreaming.

"Looking good!"

She propped herself up on her elbows and open her eyes.

It was him!

A sliver of excitement went up her spine.

She gave him a dazzling smile. "Thank you!"

He slowed the boat to a crawl. He was all alone. He was drinking her in. "Want a ride?"

She blushed and looked around. "Alright!" She was treading dangerous water, but she couldn't help it.

She wrapped a towel around her waist and stepped onto the boat.

"What a great day for a ride, thank you!" Their eyes met. "I'm Connie." She extended her hand.

"Dickie."

They shook hands and she felt a charge go through her.

He couldn't help but ogle her. "I've wanted to stop so many times, but... I don't know," he told her charmingly.

"No, I know." She laughed and took a seat — not too close to him.

They set off at a leisurely pace.

"So ... um, where do you live?"

"Over there, on the other side of the point."

"Lots of nice houses over there."

"Yeah, everyone's building bigger houses here, every year a new renovation."

She nodded. "True."

"Would you like a drink? How about a refreshing hard lemonade?" His green eyes twinkled.

She grabbed the bottle. "Thanks."

He ran a hand through his gorgeous dark hair. "So, I don't know your situation ... " he stammered. "I don't want to get you into trouble."

She nervously fiddled with her towel. "Yes, I am married," she honestly supplied, "but he's not here too often. He is a long-distance trucker."

"Ah, I see." He sipped his drink.

"Besides, there's no harm in one boat ride." She crossed her toned, tan legs.

Their eyes met. There was a crackle of sexual tension already.

He raised his bottle in the air. "Absolutely not." He had a devilish glint in his eye.

Conversation came surprisingly easy between the two strangers. They talked about the people they knew on the lake and dabbled in a bit of gossip.

All too soon they had made one revolution around the lake. She felt so comfortable and recharged around him that she hated to get off but felt that she should.

"I better go," she said, sounding a little dejected.

He was reluctant to see her go, as well. "I suppose so." He sighed. "We don't need tongues wagging."

She tittered lightly. "That's for sure."

He pulled up to her dock and aligned his boat, so she could easily step off.

She rose. Their eyes met and held for a moment. "Thank you so much."

"Anytime." He flashed his engaging smile again. "Thank you. If you want to, we can do it again."

She played with her hair. "Umm ... yeah ... we'll see."

"I understand." He nodded.

She stepped off and turned toward him. "Bye."

"See you later."

She watched him drive away. "Whoo! That was the most fun I've had in a long time," she told herself excitedly as she dove into the lake to cool herself off — and not just from the heat!

A few days later he came by again — with a bunch of passengers.

She knew some of them, so she decided to go for a spin. Besides, it looked better to go with a bunch of people.

She conversed with many of them, but she and Dickie only had eyes for each other. The air sizzled between them.

After that, she found herself lingering by the water, as often as she could, for no particular reason, just hoping he would come by.

One day, around sunset, he did. She was sitting at the edge of the dock, dipping her legs in the water, enjoying a cocktail.

"So, we meet again," he called to her, a big grin on his face.

"Hey there!"

"How about a sunset cruise?"

"Ah ... alright." She rose and got ready to step on.

He pulled up and once again helped her aboard. Electricity went through them.

"Your husband at work?"

"Yes. And my kids are at their friends' houses," she supplied.
"Nice."

They very slowly cruised along and chatted amiably.

She finished her highball. He refilled it. They watched the sunset and enjoyed each other.

"Beautiful night." She sighed.

"That's not all that's beautiful," he replied in a low voice, his eyes boring into her.

She felt herself getting warm. "Thank you."

He anxiously rubbed the back of his neck and blew out a breath.

"So ... um ... what is your situation?" he probed. "I'm sorry, I shouldn't get into this ... I can't help it..." he trailed off, shaking his head.

"No, no, that's fine," she soothed and paused. "The truth is — my marriage isn't that great." She frowned. "But it's too hard to leave at this point in time."

He nodded. "I see."

"I'm sorry. I didn't mean to lead you on."

"No, you didn't," he protested, giving her a warm smile. "I started this."

She gazed at the sky. She was quiet for a few minutes. Then she spoke again. "I think you're a wonderful guy." She unconsciously reached out and touched his knee. "You've made me feel like an attractive, desirable woman again." She kept her hands on him as her eyes searched his face.

He placed his hand on hers. "I am very attracted to you," he earnestly disclosed.

She blushed. "I ... I like you, too."

"Do you want to go see my house?" His eyes darkened with desire.

She exclaimed, "I'm not hopping into bed with you!"

He shook his head. "No, I know. I just thought you might want to see it."

"Not after dark. It doesn't look good."

"But that's when nobody would see you."

She tossed back her head and laughed. "On this lake? I'm sure somebody would see us."

"True," he agreed.

They finished their sunset cruise and reluctantly said goodnight.

One afternoon, Connie was feeling lonely and bored once again, so she decided to take her kayak out and paddle around. She found herself heading for the point.

Staying just beyond the docks, she spied a sea foam green party boat. Her heart raced.

His house was beautiful, very modern, lots of sliding glass doors, a big stone patio. She lingered by his dock for a little while, trying not to look too obvious. She didn't see him.

"Oh well," she told herself, "probably for the best." She started to paddle away. Just then he came from around the side of his house, holding a gas can.

"Hey, you!" he called out.

Connie turned and smiled as he made his way onto the dock. "Lovely house."

"Thanks. Nice to see you."

They locked eyes for a moment, then he hopped on his boat with the gas can and begin filling the tank.

She floated around his dock, looking around to see if they were being observed. She didn't see anyone.

He finished gassing up the boat. "Would you like to see my house now?" he offered with a grin.

She looked around again uneasily. "We probably shouldn't."

He surveyed the area. "No one's around. Just come in for a quick look."

She hesitated and made a face.

"Oh, alright." She beached the kayak, and they made their way into the house.

But someone's eyes are always watching.

They stepped in and she was quite impressed. Modern kitchen, high-end stainless-steel appliances, beautiful brown leather furniture. Masculine and tasteful.

"It's gorgeous in here," she raved.

"Thanks." He was grabbing two beers.

"I better not."

"Just one beer." He gestured to the couch. "Sit."

She sat, a little on edge.

They enjoyed the beautiful view of the lake.

"How many people can enjoy a vista like this?" he enthused.

She sipped her beer. "Oh, I know, we are lucky."

The lake breeze ruffled her hair prettily. She could smell his spicy cologne. The air was thick with anticipation.

"Thank you for coming over," he said softly, smoothly as he played with a tendril of her silky brown hair.

They faced each other. She gazed into his green eyes. "I ... I couldn't help myself," she admitted.

That was it. They melted into each other's arms, hungrily kissing, touching, stroking and reveling in the moment.

He reached to pull off her tank top.

"No, I can't." She pulled away abruptly.

He sighed and put a hand through his hair. "OK, I know it's wrong."

She fixed herself and got up. "I gotta go."

"I know." He frowned.

They walked down to the lake.

"Well, I'll see you around," she lamely told him.

He blew out a breath. "Yeah, of course."

She eased into her kayak and paddled away, a lump was in her throat.

Days later, as she came in from work, she encountered her husband, relaxing in his recliner, with a face like thunder. Her stomach knotted up.

"Hi babe," she greeted him enthusiastically, faking a smile.

"Don't act so sweet," he snarled, downing his whiskey. His icy stare tore into her.

She put a hand to her chest. "What?"

"A little bird told me you've been getting pretty damned friendly with Dickie Spencer," he harshly accused.

She gasped. "No ... not really ... I ... I did have a boat ride — with a bunch of other people," she hastily added.

He bolted from his chair and pushed her against the wall.

She winced and turned her face from him.

"You're lying!" he growled. "You were seen at his house! Look at me! Do you deny it?"

Shit, she thought. "OK! I was there!"

He slapped her. "You cheating bitch!"

"I wasn't doing anything wrong!" she sobbed. "It was the middle of the day! You think I'm so stupid as to mess around so carelessly?"

"It wouldn't surprise me," he bit back.

"I went in briefly — I'm sure your spies blew it out of proportion," she replied sarcastically.

His breath was hot on her face and smelled of whiskey. "And why?"

"Just to see his house."

He pulled her hair and harshly commented, "That's the best you can do?"

At that moment, one of their children came through the door.

He moved away from her and poured another drink.

I have to get away, she vowed to herself. The day after, she kayaked into the cove, a marshy, lily pad filled section of the lake only suitable for small watercraft, canoes, paddleboats, etc. It was very secluded. She enjoyed the solitude, she could relax and indulge in nature and quiet. She paddled through the swampy water, going deeper in. She watched a blue heron take flight.

She went around the bend and saw someone in a small boat fishing, a man. She didn't want to disturb him, or risk being attacked, so she started to turn and paddle away. The man turned and finally noticed her.

"Connie!"

She glanced at the man. "Dickie!" Her eyes lit up.

"Oh, this can't be a coincidence!" he exclaimed.

She sidled up to his boat. "It is nice to see you." She gave him a tight smile.

"What's wrong?"

"My husband found out about our visit." She frowned, looking a little scared.

"Oh shit, I'm so sorry." He searched her face. He then noticed a red bruise on her face, that she couldn't quite hide with makeup.

Gasping, his face became a mask of rage. "He hit you!"

She started to weep quietly. "Yes. He does once in a while."

"What? Why do you stay?"

She wiped her eyes with her hand. "I ... I can't leave right now." She shifted her eyes away.

He caressed her cheek. "Yes, you can always leave."

"Please. I can't get into it right now," she pleaded. "Just let me have this time with you."

He reached over and kissed her cheek tenderly. He then looked around.

"Go over there where it is low and sandy and step out of your kayak."

She did as she was told. He followed, and she stepped into his vessel, while he tethered her kayak to his boat.

She took the bench seat next to him and looked at him, a sad look on her lovely face.

He stroked her silky hair. She hugged him tightly, then kissed his neck. They faced each other and began kissing slowly, softly, then passionate, tongues entwined.

He pulled her onto his lap, raining soft kisses down her neck, across her chest, to her cleavage.

She moaned and moved against him.

He reached behind her back and unhooked her bikini.

She gasped and held her top on. "Right here?"

His eyes were hot with desire. "I haven't seen anyone come in but you!"

She laughed and threw her head back. "You'd say that anyway," she playfully teased.

"We are so far back here ... " He kissed her. "No one is going to see."

She groaned sexually and let her top fall away.

He sweetly massaged, kissed and licked her breasts, while slowly rubbing her private bits through her bikini bottom. She was completely turned on and reached for the zipper of his shorts and teased his manhood.

His body responded to her hand. He briefly lifted her off of him and eased his shorts and boxers down as she removed her bikini bottom and straddled him on the boat bench.

They both made sounds of pleasure as he entered her. She rode him hard.

Excitement was heightened to a feverish pitch by the thrill of having illicit sex outside and risking being caught.

Waves of pleasure coursed through them as they both peaked.

They kissed sensually.

"Thank you," she purred in his ear.

"No, thank you." He sighed contentedly as she reluctantly got off of him and they redressed.

They laughed together and enjoyed some sweet talk before they decided that they had better go.

"I don't know when I'll see you again," she sadly told him. "We have to be very discreet."

He nodded. "I know." He kissed her one more time. "You can leave first. I'll wait about a half hour."

"Alright." She stroked his leg as he motored towards the shore so she could easily get back in her kayak.

He helped her out and untethered the kayak. "Bye, babe." She blew him a kiss, then paddled away.

"See ya!" he called.

Sometime later, she was swimming at her house with her children when he passed by. She quickly turned away and pretended not to know him, and he stared straight ahead. But both smirked to themselves and felt a thrill.

As she was paddle boating in the middle of the lake one afternoon, a party boat cruised by, at close range, but at a pretty good clip. She glanced at the driver. It was Dickie.

"Meet at the Y camp tonight, 9 o'clock if you can," he quickly told her as he nonchalantly passed by without slowing down.

She gave him a thumbs-up and laughed.

As it turns out, there was a Y camp on the lake, conveniently about a 10-minute walk for them both, a perfect spot for their romps, as it wasn't always full of children, and it had a few cabins with beds in it, that were unlocked.

She could tell her children that she was having a drink at a neighbor's house, which she has many times, so that wasn't out of the ordinary.

When they couldn't meet at the Y camp, they met at a house that was being built, with no doors and windows installed, but the walls and floors were in, so that was good enough!

She was having the time of her life, getting used to all the subterfuge and sneaking around — even got so comfortable that she invited him over for a midnight skinny dip.

He quietly, furtively canoed over and fastened it to her dock.

"Hey gorgeous," he greeted her anxiously with a hot, long kiss as they divested each other of their clothes and ever so quietly waded into the warm, bath-like water.

They frolicked and quietly cooed like lovesick teenagers — until the house spot light came on and shone onto the lake.

"Oh my God! My husband is home!" she panicked, as she held her hands over her mouth.

Dickie's green eyes widened. "Shit!" He quickly swam under the neighbor's dock.

Connie tried to calm herself as she swam around, waiting for the shit to hit the fan.

Moments later, Walter emerged from the darkness, into the beam of light on the dock.

"Enjoying your late-night dip — all alone?" he asked harshly.

She could tell he was boiling. His fists were clenched.

Oh shit, why did I do this? she frightfully asked herself.

"Of course, darling — the water is so delightful – tepid as bath water ... I ... I couldn't resist." She tried to keep her tone even.

"Bullshit!" he growled, his voice getting louder. He stood at the edge of the dock as she swam farther away.

"For Christ sake, keep your voice down," she said in a hushed tone.

"Don't tell me what to do, you slut!" He glanced at the canoe.

"And just whose boat is this?" He was yelling now. "You ignorant, careless bitch!"

Just then, the neighbor's patio lights switched on, illuminating Dickie's head under the raised dock.

"Well, well, what do you know," Walter ground out. "What a goddamned surprise. You're out here acting like a two-dollar whore with our kids in the house — you bloody disgust me!" he bellowed.

Dickie swam towards the shore and stepped on to the dock. "You lay one hand on her again, I'll fucking kill you," he threatened, coming towards Walter.

Walter grabbed an oar from the canoe. "Let's go, asshole!" He swung the oar. "I'll kill the both of you!"

"Try it, you bastard!" Dickie lunged for him. They wrestled with the oar.

"For God's sake, stop it!" she screamed, swimming quickly for the dock.

"You think you're such a big man, beating up on a woman," Dickie snarled. "You cowardly piece of shit!" They continued to wrestle with the oar.

Connie made it to the dock, standing back. "No one needs to be killed here, please — stop!" she frantically screeched.

Dickie grabbed the oar from Walter and threw it in the lake. Then the punches started to fly.

"You son of a bitch!" Walter swung and hit him in the face.

"Fuck you!" Dickie snarled as he punched him in the gut.

"Stop! Please!" Connie was hysterical.

"Mom! Dad! What's going on?" Their children were gathered on the balcony, woken by the loud commotion.

Connie gasped and turned towards her kids. "Stay up there, please!" she pleaded.

The fisticuffs continued until Dickie finally overpowered Walter and pushed him off the edge of the dock, creating a loud splash.

All this time, the neighbors were enjoying a good show, but they'd had enough and didn't want things to escalate.

"Are you people done now? We're very close to calling the cops if you don't tone it down out there," the irritated neighbor threatened.

Connie was beside herself with shame and fear. "Please stop! I'm so sorry!" She called to her neighbors, "Please don't call the police!"

Walter was emerging from the lake, mad as a hornet.

"Please Walter, for the children, let it go for now," Connie begged.

"I will never let this go!" he fumed as he menacingly came at Connie and Dickie, hugging, comforting each other.

"That's it, I'll finish this," Dickie said darkly. He went at Walter hard and cold-cocked him in the face, full of rage.

Walter went back, then collapsed in a heap, sprawled out on the dock.

They got a ski rope and hog tied his hands and feet.

"Call the cops now!" Dickie demanded to the neighbors.

Walter made quite a sight as he came to, lying on the ground tied up like an errant calf, swearing, threatening and spewing venom.

The cop even had a smirk on his face.

"Are you ready to calm down, Sir?" the officer asked, choking down a laugh.

"Go to hell!"

"That's it, let's go." The cop began untying him. "A night in the cooler might straighten you out."

He was untied and cuffed, the whole sorry scenario being watched by their kids, and the neighbors.

To say that Connie was mortified was the understatement of the year. She had to press charges and take out a restraining order to keep everyone safe, and file for divorce.

But, one day, Walter showed up at the house.

"Oh God, no," she whispered to herself, shaking, as she looked out the window.

"Let's go children! Into the car!" They hurriedly went through the garage and into the auto. She could hear Walter yelling and cursing.

"Here we go." She opened up the garage door and began backing out.

As she entered the driveway, Walter hopped on the hood, banging and flailing like a madman.

"You bitch! You can't do this to me!"

She frantically reached for her phone and called the police.

"Get off the car, you raging lunatic!" she screeched. "I just called the cops!"

"Fuck you bitch!"

She put her phone on to record him.

"I've got you now, you demented piece of shit!" She showed him the phone through the windshield. "I've got enough ammo now, you are toast!"

She drove backwards and forwards trying to shift him off. "Get off the damn car!"

The kids were getting hysterical. "Dad! Please! Don't do this!" his daughter pleaded.

Connie finally backed out swiftly into the road and stopped. It was quite the terrifying tableau. Fed up, she gunned the engine backward hard, then ahead, and slammed on the brakes, not caring now if she killed him. The jarring momentum finally shook him off. He landed in a heap.

"My leg!" was the last thing she heard as she quickly reversed into her driveway, then drove in the opposite direction of her demonic husband seeking safe harbor at Dickie's, not caring nor hanging around to see if he was injured.

Chapter 12

Happy July 4th

When Mary got up, the sun was splitting the blue skies. It was Saturday, the 4th of July. The heat in the bedroom upstairs was intense. The only relief was the lack of humidity in the air. Bill was an early riser and Mary could smell the coffee brewing downstairs. She loved her morning coffee and to have it made for her was even better. She rushed downstairs.

"Morning!" she exclaimed to Bill and their two dogs, Laddy and Salty. "Looks like it's going to be a nice one! How's my babies?" she cooed to Laddy and Salty, stroking them at the same time. "And how is my darling husband today?" she whispered into Bill's ear stroking his face lovingly.

"Doing great! So far so good." Bill kissed her gently on the mouth.

They were having a barbecue today. It was going to be great one especially as this year the Fourth of July fell on a Saturday. The day's activities expanded in Mary's mind and made her smile.

"Do we have enough gas for the boat?" she asked.

"I've already been out and filled up the boat with gas and I have 10 gallons to spare," he answered.

They had purchased a brand-new Ski Nautique last summer and were dying to water ski today.

"Do we have the ropes and tube ready? What about the banana boat and the kayaks, paddles, and life preservers? Is the floating trampoline set up? Do we have enough chairs? Enough tables? Is there enough gas in the barbecue grill?" Mary liked to be organized.

"Yes, yes, yes, yes, to everything. I've got everything under control. We're ready," said Bill.

What could be better than living on the lake at this time of year? Waterskiing, swimming, drinking, fishing, eating, knee-boarding, kayaking, good weather and good friends! Mary thought and smiled again.

"Do you know what time Ray is having the fireworks?" she asked.

"He told me he is going to start once it gets dark, around 8 o'clock," Bill responded.

Ray always had great show. Last year his fireworks were the best on the lake. It seemed like there was a mini competition going on between some of the guys and their fireworks displays.

Who needed to go into Boston when Ray and his buddies were stroking their pyromaniac tendencies? she thought. "Is he going to have a floating dock like last year?"

"Yeah, and now he can do it all remotely too. He dropped ten grand this year, so it's going to be a big one!" Bill whooped in anticipation of the show.

"Okay, I'm going to check out the food situation now, and get things rolling," she said.

Mary was a bit of a gourmet cook and loved to show off her skills. The 4th of July was an annual event of gastronomic delights. Everyone brought along a dish to add to the feast.

"Put some music on please," she wheedled.

"Righty oh, honey." Within seconds, Bill had some Van Morrison playing through all the speakers in the house.

Mary danced around her kitchen, removing marinated vegetables and beef tips from the fridge and skewered them elaborately while dancing. Bill was watching with much amusement and a stirring in his loins.

"What time you think people will arrive?" she asked.

"I told everybody to come after 1 PM, so we have a little time to relax before the party begins. Woo hoo!" He grabbed her and encircled her with his arms.

"Okay sweetie, let me get my act together first," she chastened him, "then we'll begin the pre-party."

People started arriving just after 1pm as scheduled. Bill and Mary had an eclectic group of friends. They were an assorted group from all walks of life, artists, doctors, engineers, carpenters, scientists, construction workers, financiers, and musicians. Their friends usually brought other friends, visitors or family members, and so the group circle expanded exponentially. It was a true multicultural and multigenerational party event. Everyone was welcome at Mary and Bill's 4th of July lake party.

Ruairí and Maeve arrived first with their Irish entourage, Gareth and Sean who were visiting from Dublin, along with a case of the best wine, and beer. Maeve carried in her delicious risotto salad and set it on the kitchen island. It was the best salad Mary had ever had and she was envious of Maeve's culinary skills.

"I'm so glad you're here!" Mary hugged Maeve and Ruairí.

"Dia dhuit," gruffed Ruairí, followed by Maeve.

"Dia is Muire duit," said Gareth and Sean looking sheepishly at Mary.

"When are you ever going to give me the recipe for this salad?" Mary demanded of Maeve. "I love it." She had constantly asked the same question of Maeve for years and had never gotten an answer.

"It's an old family recipe." Maeve waved off the compliment. "I will email it to you."

"Welcome!" Mary said to the two young Irish lads, Gareth and Sean. Someone was Ruairí's nephew although she didn't quite catch if it was Gareth or Sean when they were introduced.

"Make yourselves at home!" She shook their hands vigorously.

"Thanks very much for having us! You have a great place here!" the two young boys replied in unison.

"Why don't you head on down to the lake and relax?" Mary indicated to the lake shore.

"Sound! Come on lads let me show you the lake," said Ruairí. They headed outside to the lakeside patio. "Bring the cooler too!" he commanded of his nephew and friend.

More people were arriving, and Mary focused her attention on her friend Jakov and his companion, an ostentatious young lady with an excessively large hat and flowery dress.

"Hey!" Mary said, "great to see you Jakov!"

Jakov was a Croatian chemist, divorced from his wife after she had an affair with her boss. It was a sad story really. The wife had gone to Croatia with their three kids for a holiday but never set foot again in the United States. That was over three years ago. Jakov had been traumatized over the whole affair. Not seeing his children upset him the most. She had seen it coming and tried to warn him that his wife was having an affair, but he had dismissed the notion of his innocent child bride doing something so uncharacteristic.

"This is Meredith," Jakov introduced the huge hatted woman to Mary.

"Nice to meet you. Love your hat!"

Meredith responded with a smile and said nothing. There was an awkward silence as the two women stared at each other.

"Ruairí and Maeve are here with some Irish people. Go and join them down at the lake!" Mary encouraged them and off they waltzed arm in arm to the lake.

Mary shook her head thinking quietly, *That's one unusual lady. Good luck! I wonder if she knows he's gay?*

Jakov had kept his homosexual tendencies secret for many years and Mary expected that he would continue to do so for a while longer.

But it couldn't last, she mused.

Next to arrive were Jane and Janice. Jane held her annual 4th of July trifle gingerly.

"Hey Mary, can I put this in the fridge please?"

"Oh my God it's beautiful, strawberries, blueberries whipped cream, and ladies' fingers! You've outdone yourself once again!" Mary looked forward to Jane's trifle annually.

"Come on in Janice, welcome!" Mary embraced her warmly.

Janice was an old friend. She had previously married and had one child, a boy. Her husband had left her, desolate when the baby was just 12 weeks old claiming some nonsense about not being able to stand the baby crying and needing space. He was a real loser, and she was better off without him, especially since she'd met Jane. Jane had also been married but her husband had passed away in their first year together. She was fortunate not to have any kids, only a giant Irish wolfhound. Mary introduced the two women 10 years earlier and they fell in love. Janice's child, Ty, was now 12 years old and came running through the door with the wolfhound, Bell, in tow much to Mary's dismay.

"Auntie Mary, can I go swimming now?" Ty jumped up and down circling her. He was a vivacious 12-year-old who was always on the move.

"That's up to your mom, but why don't you put on your swimming suit and get ready!" Mary laughed and watched him run off to change.

"Should I put this outside?" Janice was holding a huge tray of chicken wings she had cooked for the occasion.

"Let me grab one first and then bring them downstairs to the others. Yours are always the best wings Janice," said Mary.

"Why thank you darling." Janice batted her eyelids flirtatiously at Mary.

"Come on Janice, let's join the crowd!" Jane took her hand as Ty in his bathing suit and the wolfhound galloped off in front of them towards the lake.

It was 3 o'clock, and by now the party was in full swing, 30-40 people were there. Mary had brought the food to be barbecued to the lakeside patio. So many other people had arrived that she had not greeted yet. She looked around approvingly at her Italian friends Gene and Ava with their 2 kids, Mark and Penelope, an Australian couple, Chris and Laura, both Swiss doctors, Sue and Chuck, paleontologists from the good old southwest USA, and her English friends, Hermione and Fred with their kids.

"Hey Bill, it's a UN convention!" said Mary over the music blasting.

"What a way to celebrate the 4th!" he replied.

"I'll drink to that!" Jakov had a tray of vodka shots he was offering around.

"Bill, did the Gerri get here yet?" Mary said.

"Not yet," he responded.

Mary was asking about Leo, her handsome German soccer player friend, but he was a no show. *That's good*, thought Mary to herself, *he'd be a definite distraction*, and she had some partying to do.

Everyone was eating, drinking and having a blast. Bill had done a fantastic job with the kebabs. His best friend Tony had helped of course. Tony was always great with the barbecue. He and his wife Barbara used to live on the lake too, but they moved away only just last year to a large mansion in the woods with an indoor pool. It was beyond Mary and Bill's reasoning as to why they had moved away from the lake, but the Olympic size pool was certainly a draw. They remained close friends still and Bill and Tony texted each other daily.

"Hot dogs and hamburgers are ready for the kids," Bill stated.

Janice jumped up to get a hot dog. "I've been dying for this all year!" She promptly bit into one.

The kids were swimming and snorkeling. They immediately ran up to grab some food, wolfed it down and ran back to the water and jumped in.

"Hey, Mary! Can Janice and I take the canoe out?" Jane was standing with oars in hand.

"Sure, as long as you take the wolfhound with you. She only listens to you guys. I'll keep an eye on Ty," Mary said.

"Great," said Jane, "come on Janice, Bell come here!"

The two women loaded up the canoe with oars, drinks and Bell, the wolfhound and paddled off up along the shore line to do a lap around the lake.

"Who wants to water ski?" said Bill.

A few people joined in replying and Bill loaded up the boat.

"That's all I can take legally, I'll come back for more in a while," he said.

The brand-new ski boat purred leisurely out into the lake. The lake was a bit rough as there was loads of people on the lake hosting parties. Mark was the first one to go skiing. He was an expert and was built for it really. His tall muscular body sailed out the water easily on one ski and as the boat gained momentum, he started showing off somewhat. His wife Penelope yelled encouraging words from the boat.

"Yeah, Mark. Brilliant! Put some shrimp on that barbie!"

Bill was ever so slightly jealous of Mark as he watched him in the rear-view mirror of the boat effortlessly going around buoy after buoy in the slalom course. Bill cranked up the speed as Mark went past the last buoy of the course and turned sharply. Bill was testing Mark's skills, but Mark decided to let go of the rope at the last minute to save being whipped around like a little dog on a leash.

"Had enough then mate?" Bill guided the boat towards Mark floating in the water.

"Yep, I'm done. Give someone else a go." He climbed up the ladder into the boat.

Penelope was donning the skis and lifejacket as quick as she could at the stern of the boat.

"Come on Bill, take me round the lake," she said as she jumped into the water. "Wow, it's nice in here!" Bill turned the boat around heading up the lake. "OK, let's go, ready!" she yelled to Bill.

As he accelerated, she popped up easily from the water and skimmed the water's surface effortlessly. Bill admired her figure in the rearview mirror.

That is one beautiful, Australian, female, he thought, and he smiled giving her the thumbs up signal.

Mark sat watching his wife ski behind the boat. He noticed Bill signaling to her and enjoyed the fact that he appreciated her skill and beauty. They were approaching the house to drop Penelope off at the dock. Bill accelerated, rounding the turn and headed towards the house but Penelope was still holding the rope. She was headed right towards the floating trampoline and dock.

"Look out, look out!" people at the party started screaming and waving at Penelope. "Oh my God, no! Penelope!"

Penelope realized just in time that she was closing in on the trampoline and dock and let go of the ski rope quickly. She expertly braced for impact. She was unaware of the screams as she hit and rolled across the floating trampoline until she came to a stop.

"I'm OK!" she yelled as she sat up and extended an arm, waving at the boat and shore. She took a few breaths and again yelled, "I'm fine!"

Mary had been watching the skiing from the shore, drinking martinis with Maeve. Ruairí was telling his favorite joke.

"Martinis and tits are very similar. One is not enough, and three is one too many!" He was also commenting on his wife, who was on her second martini.

"Yes Ruairí, that's so true." She ignored her husband and continued sipping her cocktail.

"Good one, Ruairí!" Mary said, "and not to change the subject but has anyone seen Janice and Jane?" Mary questioned her guests in turn.

"No, not in a while," was the common response.

Mary maneuvered though her guests until she found someone who had spotted them.

"Yes. I just saw them heading into the cove a few minutes ago," said Ava.

"Well, that's a relief because they've been gone for over an hour. I was concerned because it's a bit choppy out there." Mary breathed a sigh of relief. She turned her head just in time to see Penelope do her circus act across the floating trampoline.

"Penelope, Penelope!" Mary screamed as she ran to the waterside.

Penelope was swimming into shore and Mary attended to her.

"Have a seat. Come up here and sit down. Are you OK?" Mary's stream of orders and questions enveloped Penelope.

"Just get me a drink please," Penelope said.

Maeve jostled up beside the two women, "Martini?"

"You read my mind!" Penelope grasped at the welcome drink. "Thanks sweetheart!"

They sat in silence for a while pondering that things could have been much worse. Bill and Mark had returned, docked the boat and Mark rushed to his wife's side.

"Are you OK? That was crazy. Did you mean to do that?" His stream of questions echoed in her ears.

"I'm fine and no. Guess I added another move to my repertoire eh?" Penelope smiled up at her husband.

"I'm so sorry," said Bill, "it's all my fault. I should have paid more attention to how close we were to shore."

"No worries mate!" She beamed a broad smile up at Bill.

"Wow, we all need a drink. Come on Mark." The two men headed over to the bar, at an attempt to forget a close call.

"Hello! Ahoy, ahoy!" said a voice coming from an incoming party boat.

Who were these people? Mary was annoyed. She didn't like party crashers and didn't know these people.

She stood up to see better and recognized Janice, Jane and the wolfhound, Bell. The canoe was straddled across the front of the party boat.

"We met your neighbors," Janice said.

"They're great," joined in Jane, and Bell barked her approval too.

"What happened?" Mary was concerned. "Bill, come help get the canoe off!"

Bill and Mark went to the dock and unloaded the canoe and the women off the party boat.

"We didn't get very far, maybe 10 houses up when Bell flipped the canoe by jumping out of it. These guys rescued us!" Janice said.

"Nightmare! We couldn't get the water out of the canoe. And then these kind people were going by and helped us out," Jane said. "They hauled us and Bell in, and loaded the canoe onto the front of their boat."

"And it would have been impolite to refuse a tour of the lake." Janice looked at their rescuers gratefully. "We had a fantastic tour. Let me introduce our heroes, Sharon and Pete Sampson, your neighbors from the cove."

Mary observed that Jane and Janice were incredibly happy and not in the slightest bit upset after their traumatic rescue. *They must have had a few on their tour,* she thought. "Hi, nice to meet you and thanks very much for rescuing my friends." She nodded gratefully at her new neighbors.

Mary had seen this couple every weekend evening at 4 o'clock motoring out of the cove in their luxurious party boat. She had often wondered about them and realized now that they were both astonishingly good looking.

"Nice to meet you too!" Pete shook Bill's hand firmly.

"Thanks, you're a star!" Bill said.

"Good on you mate!" chimed in Mark. "You're a life saver! We need some more of those around here. Don't we Bill?"

Mark was still fuming about Bill causing his wife to crash into the trampoline.

"That's right. Thanks again Pete. We must have you over for a cocktail some time." Bill eyed Sharon and winked at her. Her beauty had not been overlooked by Bill and Mark and she nodded agreeably to Pete.

"Happy 4th!" she cooed at them and the party boat reversed out onto the lake.

"That was some looker, eh Bill?" Mark jabbed Bill's side.

"You're telling me! Marilyn Monroe come on down!" he replied.

"Come on guys. Stop that! He wasn't too bad either!" Mary said. She was also in awe of the handsome couple. "Drinks all round. Now!" she cheerfully suggested, and Ruairí's joke, three tits or martinis is one too many, echoed in her head.

As they headed up to the bar for more cocktails, Mary spied some new guests that she did not know.

"Mary, my kid came over with some of his friends. I hope that's OK?" Bill's buddy Tony came over to her. He indicated to a group of young men sitting in a circle laughing and surrounding a case of beer. There must have been 6 or 7 of them.

Way too many! Mary thought.

"Sure Tony, everyone's welcome here on the 4th, right Bill?" She dragged Bill over to supervise this collection of young men who had just arrived.

It was too much for her to handle right now, and she was relieved when Bill and Tony went over to the group of young men and engaged them in conversation. She hoped they were all over 21. Tony's kid was in college, so she gave it no more thought and went off in search of Jakov whom she hadn't seen in some time.

I could use a vodka now, she thought, *where is he?*

Mary spied Jakov and Meredith kayaking near a small island at the lake's center. She happily sat down beside Gene and Ava who were chatting casually while minding all the kids swimming and jumping on the floating trampoline. Ty had made friends with their 2 girls and was completely unaware of his mother's and her companion's recent rescue by the handsome lake couple.

"And how are you Ava?" Mary asked.

"Doing great!" Ava was dishing into some of the trifle. "Can the kids go tubing or on the banana boat now?"

Mary could tell, she was fed up minding the kids and needed a break.

"Sure, I'll get Bill. You want to go too, Gene?" Mary suggested, hoping he would go and leave Ava behind.

"Sure thing, love to!" Gene got up to go. "I'll get Bill."

Gene was always amenable to everything as was his wife. They were a fun-loving Italian couple with a keen sense of fashion and loads of money. They were slightly eccentric but always up for a good time.

"Why don't you bring Chuck with you too?" Mary indicated over to Sue and her husband who had returned from excavating the mid-west in their never-ending fossil hunts.

"You want to go with the guys, Chuck? And us girls can chat?" Mary motioned for Sue to join the girl group forming.

"Sure, I'm game for anything," Chuck replied, "let's go kids."

Sue was a great guitarist and had brought her guitar to the party, which she promptly pulled out. They sat around singing for some time until Ruairí came over and started singing Irish rebel ballads which changed the mood somewhat. Mary quickly got up and put some casual music back on the speakers and spied Jakov and Meredith returning from their kayaking and went to the lake to help them in.

"This is a beautiful place here! But it's a little hectic out there in the center of the lake," Meredith stated.

"Yes, we like it," Mary said. She was still unsure of this unusual woman Jakov had brought. She had a slight accent, but Mary couldn't tell if it was real or put on.

"Come let's eat, drink and be merry!" Jakov cajoled Meredith up to the food and drinks.

Dusk was beginning to fall on the party. It would soon be time for fireworks. Mary couldn't wait. She loved being on the lake for the fireworks. The lake would be swarming with boats with their lights out anchored off shore admiring the spectacular Boston Pops-like show. They had an extra fishing boat too which might come in handy she thought to herself if they couldn't fit everyone on the Nautique.

Maybe some people would leave, and they could all go on one boat. Mary hoped that the guests with kids would head off soon and only adults would be left. *That would be for the best,* but she kept that thought to herself. *Everyone was welcome at Mary and Bill's on the 4th,* she reprimanded herself.

Bill returned with Chuck, Gene and the kids to the dock and Mary went to meet them.

"That was great. The kids had a blast!" Gene thanked her.

"I'm so happy. We had a little sing song with Sue while you were gone. That is until Ruairí started with his Irish stuff." Mary raised her eyes to heaven.

"Bet Ava loved that," Gene joked.

Everyone knew that Ava and Gene both hated Irish music with a passion. Mary was unsure if that was just because Ireland had beaten the Italians in the World Cup that year or simply because they disliked Ruairí's vocal expertise.

"I put some music on, Bill. We should think about the fireworks it's getting close to time now," Mary stated.

"We have time sweetie. Let's relax for a while. I'll cook up some more on the BBQ. We'll eat some, and then I'll get the boats ready," Bill said.

He too had thoughts about the number of people and envisioned using the bass fishing boat, in addition to the Nautique.

"Where's Tony?" Bill yelled up to the deck patio, "get the grill going!"

"Ready when you are Bill." Tony popped his head up and immediately went to the grill.

Food was prepared and eaten. Mary had made her infamous chick tikka and lamb saag with samosas and naan bread. Everyone seemed happy and excitement was brewing for the fireworks.

Ruairí extolled, "You've outdone yourself once again Mary!" He gave her a big hug and kiss. "I just love the samosas. You've got to show Maeve how to make them." The Indian food was a big hit, and it was an annual meal on the 4th which Ruairí looked forward to every year.

"Yes, I'll give Maeve that recipe once she gives me her risotto one!" Mary still had not revealed that she did not cook the samosas herself. She bought them from an Indian grocery store.

The lake had gone quiet now.

"Is it okay if I put a movie on for the kids?" asked Fred's wife, Hermione.

Mary and Bill had a home theater in their basement.

"That's a great idea," replied Mary.

"I'll stay here and mind the kids," said Hermione, who had an aversion to water, anything about it, on it, or near it.

She must have the most terrifying experience in her youth, mused Mary.

"You go on, enjoy yourself," Hermione said.

"That would be brilliant!" replied Mary. "Bill, why don't you take all the guys on the fishing boat and I'll take the rest on the Nautique?"

The group of young men who came with Tony's son, James, got up agreeably and started gathering their beer and snacks.

"I'll go with Bill too," said Tony.

That would make 8 in the fishing boat, which seemed like too many, to Mary.

"That'll work," said Bill.

The group of eight men loaded up, placing a large cooler centrally with chips and dips surroundings it.

"Off we go," said Tony to Bill.

Mary looked at the fishing boat as it lowered deeper into the water, as the 8 men boarded.

"Just go slow," Mary cautioned the men.

The water seemed perilously close to the top of the boat. But they pottered off, slowly toward Ray's house.

"Come on who's going with me?" Mary asked.

Ruairí said, "Count me in."

"Me too!" joined in Maeve.

"I can only take 7," said Mary.

Just then, their new neighbors Pete and Sharon Sampson were cruising by.

"We're going to the fireworks. Anyone want to join us? We have room," they yelled out.

It was 7:30 pm and boats were slowing moving down the lake to Ray's house. Jakov and Meredith promptly jumped on board the party boat, followed by Gene and Ava.

"That's' great, thanks," said Mary.

The Nautique filled up with the rest of the gang, Janice and Jane, Sue and Chuck, Ruairí and Maeve.

"Anyone else?" inquired Pete.

"No some have already headed down to Rays," said Mary, "and some are staying here and will watch from the shore."

"OK," said Pete, "let's motor."

They took off from the dock leisurely making their way down to the pending firework display at Ray's house.

There were at least 20 or 30 other boats there. It was hard to determine as they had their lights off but in the reflection of the fireworks on the lake, Mary estimated at least 20. She found Bill and Tony by the raucous sound of the young men laughing which echoed off the water in the small fishing boat.

"Made it OK?" Mary asked.

"No problem," said Bill smiling, and boarded the Nautique.

Pete's party boat was close by, but they had tied up to some other lake friends and Mary was reluctant to tie up alongside them. So, they anchored beside the small fishing boat, watching the incredible display dumbstruck.

Ray had certainly outdone himself this year. One after another, each firework roared and exploded into a myriad of colors. The grand finale was a huge, red, white, and blue American flag. A stars and stripes spectacular! The fireworks had gone on for nearly an hour. Boats began to cautiously maneuver their way home, but Mary waited for most of them to depart. She could see Pete's party boat in the distance headed back to her house and was anxious to get back to her guests.

"You guys ready?" she asked Bill as he loaded back onto the little boat.

It looked so small, in the dark with all those young raucous men in it.

"That was brilliant!" they all joined in thanking Bill and Mary profusely.

They were obviously a little tipsy and Mary thought they should have been thanking Ray for the fireworks, but she let that go.

"You're welcome, now, let's go" she answered. "We have got to get back to the house now. Want to race?"

"Sure," said Bill, pulling away first and opening up the throttle.

Without thinking, Mary opened the throttle on the Nautique and blasted her way down the lake. Ruairí and Maeve were whooping it up encouraging her. As she pulled up alongside the fishing boat and overtook them, the wake of the Nautique headed towards the small fishing boat. Mary turned her head, grinning broadly at the guys in the boat. Before she knew it, the young guy sitting up front, stood up, and jumped off the front of the boat, diving into the oncoming wave. His weight forced the bow of the boat into the water and when the Nautique's wake broke on top of it, the boat flipped head over heels.

Mary could not believe her eyes. She did not hear any sounds. A stillness enveloped her. She quickly stopped accelerating.

"Turn around and get them! Go get them," screamed Ruairí.

Mary was reluctant to power back as the men could be anywhere in the water. They did not have a flashlight to illuminate the water. Slowly, one by one heads appeared at the surface of the water.

"There!" yelled Ruairí pointing, "and there!" Mary steered the boat cautiously in the dark.

"This is fucking crazy get them all on this boat!" screamed Mary, "Bill! Where's Bill? Tony, where are you?"

They saw Tony as his bobbing head and flailing arms gave sound to his placement in the darkness and pulled him into the Nautique while Bill hung onto the upside-down fishing boat.

"Get in the boat, get in the boat!" Mary urgently voiced.

"Where James?" screamed Tony, scanning the water for his son.

Suddenly 2 more heads popped up, one of them was James. One by one they plucked the young men from the water.

"Do we have everybody? Is that all of them?" Mary asked.

As Mary did not even know how many friends James had brought to the house, she was asking him to ascertain if all his friends were on board. He was useless. He could hardly speak.

"Get in the boat Bill!" Mary commanded.

"No, I'm staying with the boat," he said.

"Get in the fucking boat!" Mary demanded once again, as Bill clutched onto the side of the overturned boat. Next, the cooler popped up beside him.

"No bring everyone home and come back for me in case there is anyone else out here."

Mary reluctantly and very cautiously headed the Nautique back to the house. She did not want to leave Bill alone hanging onto the side of the overturned fishing boat but understood his reasoning. Some neighbors came out with flashlights and were scanning the water for more heads. Mary dropped everyone off at home, except Ruairí who stayed with her. He was an ex-navy veteran and sat determinedly beside her. They headed back out to Bill in the middle of the lake.

"Bill!" Mary yelled out. She could not see him, and she began to panic.

"I'm here!" He swam around from the other side of the boat.

"Get in now, OK?" she said.

Bill got in and she hugged him and wrapped a towel around him while Ruairí tied up the upside-down fishing boat to the Nautique and they motored home in shocked silence.

When they got back to the house, they saw the young lads dispersed about, laying on the grass or patio in shocked silence. One of them seemed to be recovering after vomiting profusely.

He was the one who jumped off the front of the boat causing it to capsize thought Mary. *If he hadn't dove off, none of this would have happened.*

He was talking, rambling on.

"I ended up underneath the boat," he explained. "It was totally black, and I felt something at my legs. I reached down and felt something, a head so I grabbed it by the hair and pulled it up. It was James!"

"Oh my God you saved him," Mary exclaimed.

James was still sitting in stunned silence, the drunkenness wearing off, with Tony and Bill hovering at his side. Mary promptly fetched towels and Maeve went to make a pot of tea for everyone.

Mary returned with the towels. "Is everyone here? Are all of your friends here?" she questioned James and his friends, afraid that she would hear the answer she feared.

"Yeah we're all here," someone said, "but where's the Irish guy?" Mary heard a male voice ask quietly.

"Ruairí, where's your nephew and his friend?" Mary ran to him hysterical. "Did we get them?"

Ruairí was holding his nephew Gareth in his arms consoling him. "Sean was in the little boat with the other guys, he's missing."

"No!" Mary collapsed to the ground in a heap and wept.

Chapter 13

No Happy Endings

In a modest house on the lake, lives Heather Drake, mid-thirties, never married, always a party girl and down for a good time.

She is a masseuse, and the rumors are true, she will do more than just give you a good rub down if you cough up the cash.

Today she has a new client, Dale Donovan, handsome, somewhat of a pretty boy, also in his thirties. He is in pharmaceutical sales and travels a lot for his job.

He is also a sex addict.

After Heather gave him a long, relaxing massage, he handed her a nice wad of cash, and they had a wild, raucous time in the sack.

Heather loved it, as she really got off on hardcore, kinky sex, as well. She hoped she would see him again.

After leaving Heather's house, Dale went to the gym for a quick workout and a shower. Then he went home.

"Hey babe, how was your workout?" his husband asked him as he prepared the salad for dinner.

Dale grinned impishly. "Very vigorous."

After that, Dale became a regular customer of Heather's, at least once or twice a month.

During one particularly rough sex session, after they both climaxed and he pulled out, he noticed that the condom had broken.

A panicked look crossed his face. "Oh shit!"

"Don't worry, I always use backup protection," she assured him. "I'm on the pill."

He relaxed a little. "Good to know." He got out of bed and began dressing.

"Oh, by the way, I'm going away for a month — overseas to London. It's a business trip."

She playfully pouted. "Aww, that's a shame. You're my favorite client."

He put his head back and laughed easily. "I bet you say that to everyone," he teased as he zipped up his pants.

She smirked. "Not true!" She got out of bed and crossed the room naked to give him a kiss. "I really will miss you. Have a safe trip."

He caressed her breasts. "Mmm — nice." He turned and headed for the door. "See you later."

She also picked up a new female client, Liz Jacobson, an older woman, probably mid-fifties. She looked familiar, but she couldn't quite place her.

She began the massage and they made banal small talk.

"I've seen you before, I'm sure of it ... I just can't remember where." Heather paused and ruminated briefly. "You must live on the lake."

"I do. On the other side — with my husband," Liz returned. "I've also seen you at several get-togethers."

"It's quite an interesting place to live, drug busts, unexplained deaths, swinger parties. Always something to talk about." She laughed. "Pretty lively for being out in the boonies. Would make a good television show!"

Liz chuckled. "True."

They continued to gossip and laugh as Heather continued the session.

"OK, you're all set," Heather announced as she finished rubbing lavender oil into Liz's back.

"Absolutely wonderful," Liz enthused, completely relaxed. "You are really good."

"Thank you," Heather responded as she washed her hands.

"I guess I should go put my clothes back on ... I can hardly move." She sighed luxuriously.

Heather grinned. "Take your time. Relax. Enjoy the moment."

After a few moments, Liz got up and dressed. She went to her purse and got the money out to pay.

"Here you go." She handed her the money, and a sizable tip. "Worth every penny." She gazed at Heather, a little too long.

"Thank you so much." Heather took the cash, walked into the kitchen and placed it in a drawer, grateful to break eye contact. She returned and walked Liz to the door.

"Please come again." She painted a pleasant look on her face.

"Very soon," Liz promised. "Thank you, again." She walked out and got into her car.

Sure enough, a few days later she returned.

"Hi! Nice to see you again!" Heather greeted her cordially. "I guess I am really good," she humored her.

Liz stared at her. "You are. I can't get enough."

Heather prepared the work area while Liz went into the bathroom to disrobe.

She emerged from the bathroom fully naked, and casually made her way to the massage table and laid down on her stomach.

"I'm sorry. Didn't I put some towels and a robe in there?" Heather asked, unable to hide the surprised tone of her voice. She quickly covered her buttocks with a towel.

"I saw them." She grinned mischievously. "I like to be totally free sometimes. I hope I didn't shock you."

Heather laughed. "Hell, I'm a masseuse, I've seen it all." She began the session.

"Any new gossip?" Liz asked.

"Umm — actually, yes." She was working the knots out of Liz's shoulders. "Allegedly there's some weirdo going around peeking into women's windows. He's naked but wears some ghastly mask. Sometimes he's masturbating."

Liz gasped. "Are you for real?"

"That's what I heard." She worked oil into the small of her back. "From very credible women — not drunks or mentally unstable or anything." She chuckled.

Liz sighed. "On this lake, I guess anything goes!" She shook her head.

"Yup."

"Which side of the lake?"

"I guess various spots all over."

"Oh geez, wonderful."

They continued to breezily chat. The appointment flew by.

She finished with a soothing hand massage. "Feel better?" Heather asked stepping away to put the oil on the shelf.

Liz sat up and stretched like a contented cat, her breasts fully exposed.

"Excuse me, I have to use the bathroom," Heather announced and left the room.

When she returned, Liz was still lounging on the massage table, fully exposed, having removed the towel from her nether regions.

She must be an exhibitionist, Heather thought. "You can use the bathroom now."

Liz didn't move, just continued making eye contact with a peculiar look on her face.

"Everything OK?" she queried.

"Just fine." She gave Heather an engaging smile.

Heather looked puzzled. "Umm — alright." She turned and headed for the kitchen.

"Can I talk to you for a minute?" Liz asked apprehensively.

"Of course." She slowly came towards Liz.

"I ... uh ... " she stammered and looked away.

"What is it?" Heather coaxed.

Liz nervously brushed her hair away from her face. "I heard through the grapevine that uh — you do a little extra — for the right price."

Heather's eyebrows shot up. "That's true."

Liz blushed and cleared her throat. "Well, the thing is ... I've never been with a woman." She fidgeted with her earring. "I'd like to try it." She looked sheepishly at Heather and continued. "You see, my husband is a wimpy, soft-talking non-manly man." She shrugged her shoulders. "He's never been good in bed," she honestly admitted. "But he's decent and kind, so I stay with him."

Heather nodded. "I see."

"So, name your price." She smiled at Heather. "Please do this for me."

Heather was quiet for a moment. "OK, I'll do it," she acquiesced.

Liz's face brightened. "Great! Thank you so much!"

They agreed on a price and headed for the bedroom where Heather gave her a fantastic roll in the hay. Liz was a little older than what she would go for, but she gave enthusiastically in the sack. Good money is good money!

Afterwards, they languished in bed, sapped and satisfied.

"Amazing!" Liz stated. "My husband has never been able to satisfy me like that."

"Perhaps you've been a lesbian all this time, but tried to be straight to avoid the stigma," Heather informed her. "Not that being gay is a big deal anymore," she hastily put in.

Liz stared at the ceiling. "Maybe."

"Or you're bisexual?"

"Are you bisexual?" Liz probed.

Heather pondered the question. "I guess I am." She laughed. "Good to be multifaceted."

They laughed together.

Liz became a very frequent customer, and Heather enjoyed the hefty payout, and the sex. Under her tutelage, Liz became a thrilling lover.

Time went by, and she realized that she hadn't seen Dale for a while. She did miss him, he was a voracious, hot lover. *Perhaps he's still abroad on business*, she thought.

As it seems to happen sometimes, you think of someone and they uncannily materialize.

She was pumping gas one day when coincidently so was Dale.

They waited in line together to pay.

"Dale! how are you?" She happily greeted him. "Long time, no see."

A weird look crossed his face, but he quickly recovered.

"Heather! Hello!" He flashed a grin. "I know. I've been busy traveling for work. I'm sorry." He gave her a quick hug.

She noticed he was a bit thinner. "Come over sometime, I will make you a nice home-cooked meal." She looked at him from head to toe.

Another undiscernible expression came over his face, then vanished. "I do need one." He rubbed his stomach. "I don't eat very well while traveling. Things get hectic."

She nodded. "I'm sure."

He paid for his gas and turned to leave. "I will be in touch." He patted her shoulder and rather curtly left.

"OK. Bye," she called to his retreating figure.

He never did get in touch with her.

She was busy with her other clients, especially Liz.

One afternoon, Liz showed up, completely hysterical.

"What's the matter?" Heather asked her distraught friend.

Liz was wiping tears from her eyes. "Someone knows about us," she sniffled.

Heather's eyes widened. "What? What are you talking about?" She rubbed Liz's hand.

Liz pulled away, went to her purse and took out an envelope. "Someone knows."

She handed the envelope to Heather. Inside were photos of the two of them — in extremely indelicate positions.

Heather gasped. "What the hell?" She shook her head as she went through the photos.

Liz started sobbing again.

"Someone stood outside my bedroom window and snapped these?" Heather remarked, incredulous. "I can't believe it."

"I know." Liz stood up and started pacing anxiously. "And now they're blackmailing me."

"Seriously?"

Liz was staring at the lake. "I didn't tell you that my husband is a powerful local politician, and a scandal like this would destroy him." Tears welled up in her eyes again. "I can't do that to him."

Heather ran a hand through her hair. "Oh no. I'm so sorry."

"They want $10,000."

"Shit! What are you going to do?"

Liz came and sat on the couch. "I have to pay it." She sighed wearily.

"You can get your hands on that kind of cash? Without your husband's knowledge?"

"Yes. I have my own account."

"Thank goodness." Heather shook her head sympathetically. "Any idea who could be doing this?"

Liz shrugged her shoulders. "It could be anyone. Politicians always have a ton of enemies and people out to get them. It comes with the job."

"That's true."

Liz put her head in her hands. "I can't believe this. I was so stupid and careless. I could ruin my husband!" she wailed as she wiped her eyes with a tissue.

"It must be someone familiar with the lake because they want the money placed on the island after 10 PM."

Heather's brow furrowed. "Oh really? Yeah, I guess you would have to know the lake to be aware of the island." She gave her friend a wan smile. "Well, that's a tiny clue." She rubbed her forehead and went on. "How do you know they won't keep some photos? With cell phones and the Internet these days, they could spread like wildfire."

Liz frowned. "I know. I have no idea if they'll spread them. What the hell am I supposed to do? I have to pay and see what happens."

"I'm so sorry. Would you like a drink or something?"

Liz rose off the couch. "No thank you. I gotta get out of here. I just wanted to tell you what's going on." She headed for the door.

"What a pathetic world this is. Such a shame." Heather disgustedly pursed her lips.

Liz's face was pale. "I know." She fished her keys from her purse. "I'll let you know how it goes."

"Thank you." She patted her Liz's shoulder. "Good luck."

About a week later, Liz came back to visit Heather. They were on the deck, having a glass of wine.

"So, how did it go?" Heather asked anxiously. "Are you OK?"

Liz was puffing on a cigarette. "Everything went well, I guess." She flicked the ashes. "I left the money there — didn't inform the cops — and that was it." She shrugged. "I haven't heard anything again."

"Well, that's good. I hope that's the end of it."

"Me too." She sipped her wine. "So far my husband has no idea."

"Awesome." Heather raised her wine glass. "Cheers."

They clinked glasses. "Cheers."

They finished the bottle of wine while affably chatting.

"I could really use a massage after all the hell I've been through lately," Liz announced while stretching her neck. "Just a massage — nothing else." She gave Heather a thin smile.

"I'm sure you need one after this ghastly nightmare." Heather rose to prepare the work area. "This one's on the house."

"Great! Thank you so much." She stood up and headed for the bedroom to disrobe.

While in the bedroom, she noticed the bed was full of clothing, mostly new, with the price tags still on them, ready to be packed into an open suitcase. After a little more snooping, she found two plane tickets and an itinerary for a Mediterranean cruise with two passports — Heather and Luke Grey's — her lover who just lost his wife Estelle, to an accident on the lake.

Liz's wheels started turning in her head. Something told her to look in the closet.

She opened the fold away doors, and sure enough, she recognized the navy-blue duffel bag in the corner of the closet, thrown in amongst other totes, satchels and handbags. The very same duffel bag she put the ransom money in.

"Son of a bitch!" she said to herself, starting to shake with rage. *She's the blackmailer!* she thought, while starting to frantically pace the room. *I don't believe this!* She futilely tried to calm herself by taking a few deep breaths. She regained a little composure and headed out of the bedroom.

Heather's back was to her as she quietly crossed from the bedroom to the kitchen and eased a knife out of the cutlery block.

"Taking an impromptu cruise?" Liz calmly said to Heather, as she was placing a towel on the massage table.

Heather jumped at the sound of her voice and flung around to face her. "My goodness! You startled me! I didn't hear you come over!" She placed a hand on her chest. "Why are you still dressed?"

A wild look was in Liz's eyes. "I decided I shouldn't really linger around here anymore, after that horrific shakedown."

Heather looked uneasy as hell. "But we're not doing anything sexual." She forced a laugh.

"You didn't answer my question. You're taking a cruise?"

Heather's eyes became shifty. "Yes, yes I am." She swallowed hard. "I've always wanted to see the Med."

Liz let out a sarcastic chuckle. "Who doesn't? Pretty expensive, eh?"

"Very."

"Been saving a long time?"

"Yeah. I have. But uh… business has been good lately."

"Indeed," Liz harshly replied.

They were face to face and uncomfortably close.

Liz's eyes darkened. "It was you."

Heather's heart raced as she tried to move away.

In an instant Liz brandished a razor-sharp chef's knife and held it to Heather's stomach. "Try to move and I'll slide this right through you," she menacingly stated.

Heather's eyes widened in sheer terror. "What are you doing? What are you talking about?"

"It all adds up now. How could I not know?" She held the knife steadily to her midsection. "You're the blackmailer. It's perfect." She continued in a low, eerie tone. "You know the lake, you know the island, and I'm always here. The photos were taken at your house." Her face became a mask of hatred. "How bloody convenient."

Heather shook her head. "You're wrong, Liz. Please calm down and put the knife down."

"You're a despicable whore!" she screeched. "How could you do this!"

"Liz! please! You're going off the rails here! You don't want to do this!" she pleaded. "I would never betray you!"

"Bullshit!" She was an inch from her face. "I saw the duffel bag, you stupid bitch! That's a pretty rookie move, you ignorant slut!" she barked. "Keeping the damn ransom bag! I guess you haven't done this before!"

Heather gasped. "Oh my God!" She started crying. "I'm so sorry, Liz! Please, you don't want to do this!" she hysterically repeated.

"Someone needs to teach you a lesson."

Heather grabbed the knife to try to knock it out of Liz's hand.

"You twisted bitch!" she screamed as they wrestled with the weapon, but Liz had a firm grasp on it. She plunged it into Heather's stomach.

Bloodcurdling screams filled the air.

Liz gasped and pulled away from Heather, not believing what she had just done. She watched Heather grab her stomach as blood soaked through her shirt.

"My God, help me!" Heather begged as she staggered helplessly around, then collapsed to the floor.

Liz watched briefly as the woman lay dying. She gathered her belongings, wrapped the knife in paper towels and bolted for the door, in shock and disbelief. She could hear her pleading for help as she shut the front door.

On her way home, she threw the knife in the woods in a remote area. *My god, I've just killed someone!* she thought, almost vomiting on herself.

She returned home and had time to take a nice, hot shower and try to get a hold of herself before her husband came in from work. She busied herself preparing a delicious meal of short ribs, rice pilaf, and fresh summer squash from their garden when her husband arrived.

"Hi, hon, how was your day?" he greeted.

"Pretty quiet," she answered while forcing a smile, then taking a sip of wine. "And yours?"

"Same old, same old." He headed to the bedroom to take off his suit.

They were in the middle of enjoying their dinner when the doorbell rang.

"I'll get it," Liz's husband said as he rose from the table.

"OK." Liz broke out in a cold sweat. Her hand shook as she brought her wine glass to her lips.

Her husband opened the door. Two policemen were standing there.

Liz's wine glass slipped from her fingers and shattered on the floor.

"Good evening, Sir, we need to speak to your wife," an officer told him.

Her husband's face registered surprise. "Excuse me?"

The cop peered around the flabbergasted man and spied Liz. "Mrs. Jacobsen?"

"Yes."

They brushed past her husband and came towards her.

"You need to come with us."

"Why?" she shrieked. "No!"

"What the hell is going on?" her husband demanded.

162

The detective turned towards Jason. "I'm sorry, Sir, but your wife stabbed a woman today, actually it was her lesbian lover ... " He watched as Jason's face exploded into bewilderment and rage.

Jason stared at his wife. "Is this for real?"

Liz began wailing and crumpled in her chair.

"She stabbed her and left her for dead," the cop interjected. "Luckily, the poor woman's boyfriend came in just in time to save her — get her to a hospital. She was very close to dying."

Liz continued sobbing as she brought her hands to her mouth.

Her husband gaped at her, stunned silent.

"We got a full statement from Heather Drake, the woman she stabbed, identifying your wife as the perpetrator. They'd been lovers for a while," a cop supplied.

Her husband was apoplectic. "How could you do this to me?" he growled. "To us? What did I do to deserve this? You've ruined me! Our lives! Everything!"

"I'm sorry! I'm so very sorry! I hate myself!" Liz ranted and raved as she was led out of the house, arrested for attempted murder.

There were no happy endings for anyone ...

Her husband's political career crashed and burned spectacularly, as the salacious story hit the papers and was the talk of the town.

On Heather's end, the police arrested her on blackmail charges and prostitution. They got her boyfriend Luke for being an accessory for snapping pictures.

But the worst was yet to come ...

The doctor came in one day, looking grim.

"I'm sorry to tell you this, but when we cross-matched your blood for a transfusion — um ... I'm sorry ... " His tone became hushed and sympathetic.

"You have HIV."

Heather's body involuntarily sank into the bed, all life seemed to drain away for a moment as she went into shock.

She pondered for a moment, then she became lucid again. *Dale,* she agonizingly thought, and wept quietly.

Pretty soon, there was an outbreak of AIDS on the lake — from the well-to-do to the blue-collar joes, they all got infected.

No one is safe from misery and despair on Blue Lake.

Chapter 14

Phantom of the Lake

In a quaint, Cape Cod style cottage on the lake lives Francesca and Olivia Springfield, mother and daughter. Olivia, the daughter, is 36, her mother is 79, having her 2 children in her forties.

Olivia has remained single, even though she is very beautiful. Having had her share of short-term, failed relationships, she has opted to stay with her mother, which has worked out well. Most of the men she has dated have been complete disappointments, being too arrogant, posh, playboys, pill poppers, or looking for a sugar momma.

Plus, she has never wanted children. She's traveled quite extensively — with family, friends, and boyfriends. She has enjoyed being free and able to do what she wants, and fortunately her mother is still active and vital.

Being a bit reserved, they tend to keep to themselves, but do have a few neighbors with whom they have a good relationship with, and they go for an occasional boat ride.

While relaxing and enjoying the view of the lake from their deck one beautiful afternoon, enjoying their daily cocktail, Angus

McGregor came cruising by in his pontoon boat, offering a ride, as he has done summer after summer.

They have always politely declined, as he lives on the other side of the lake, and Francesca and Olivia don't know the lake people that he chums with.

At long last, they accepted the ride.

Introductions were made as they boarded the craft and found a seat.

Olivia scanned the sea of unfamiliar faces and found one she knew, Derek Murphy, who lived a few houses down from her.

"I can't believe you finally got on this boat," Angus ribbed good-naturedly.

She laughed.

"Where have you been hiding?" an unfamiliar voice piped up.

Olivia looked around to identify it. It was Danny Whitcomb, a decent-looking man in his 50s.

"We're kind of shy, quiet people," Olivia responded. "But it is nice to get out and be sociable." She blushed prettily.

"Your last name is Springfield?" Danny queried.

"Yes."

"That sounds familiar." He gazed up at the sky as he ruminated a moment. "Ah, yes, that's right, my father bought your old wooden boat years ago."

Her eyes widened in surprise. "No kidding." She chuckled. "What a small world."

"I know, right." He smiled genially. "You must have a lot of fond childhood memories of being out in it."

Olivia tossed her hair back. "Oh, I do. My dad could be a hellraiser sometimes, he liked to have a good time."

Conversation flowed easily amongst the crowd. People continued being picked up and some opted to be dropped off at their house as the craft cruised the lake.

A very pretty brunette with a long braid came aboard and offered everyone some homemade blueberry liqueur.

Many people happily imbibed. It was a very pleasant ride.

"So, Francesca, how long have you lived on the lake?" A very handsome, distinguished-looking man who was seated next to Olivia's mother, was speaking. He was Dorian Winchester.

"My husband and I moved here in 1955," she supplied. "The house was furnished — with 2 boats. We paid $10,500."

"Wow. That's amazing," Dorian returned. "The lake must have changed so much since then."

Francesca nodded. "Definitely. Not many original cottages left. So many big, beautiful new houses now."

"True."

Olivia was glancing at Dorian as he and her mother engaged in conversation. Out of the corner of her eye she knew someone was staring at her. She shifted her gaze slightly and noticed Danny's eyes boring into her. She quickly looked away.

"So, Derek, when does Kathleen return from Ireland?" Olivia asked. Derek's wife was on her annual summer trip to their homeland.

"One more week."

She shook her head wistfully. "I wish I could go."

"Maybe next year you could visit for a few days. You two would have fun, I'm sure." He smiled.

"I'll have to renew my passport. I would love to go."

They made one more trip around the lake. It was getting late. Dorian's wife opted to get off the boat, while he stayed on.

Olivia had to go to the bathroom, as they had probably been on for almost 2 hours.

"Could you drop us off next, please? I have to go to the bathroom."

"No problem," Angus replied.

They neared the house.

"You should come out for the next party boat hitch-up," Dorian suggested. "Lots of good food, mimosas, and Bloody Marys." He flashed a friendly smile.

"I could make some blueberry muffins," Francesca remarked.

"Sounds good," he said. "Hope to see you there."

"Thanks, everyone. Nice meeting new people."

Olivia and her mother rose and prepared to disembark.

Several men also got up to help her mother off the vessel, including Dorian. Olivia stood behind her mother, watching as she was assisted. Dorian stood next to Francesca making sure she didn't fall backward as she stepped onto the dock.

Then he helped Olivia, putting his arm around her waist, then moving down and grabbing her ass as she alit.

Did anyone just see that? she wondered, horrified.

It was almost 10 at night, quite dark, but the dock was illuminated by the outside patio lights.

They all said their goodbyes and the two women walked the short distance to their house.

"That was quite nice," Francesca commented as they strolled along.

Olivia nodded. "It really was. There are some decent people on this lake. Good to be sociable."

"Yes."

She let out a laugh. "That guy grabbed my ass as he helped me off the boat."

Her mother's eyes widened. "Really?" She chuckled. "That was bold."

"Yeah. I hope it doesn't get back to his wife." She frowned. "I didn't instigate anything."

"Of course you didn't."

A few days later Olivia was taking the clothes off the line when she noticed something was amiss. She was sure she hung out her pink lace underwear and bra set. She remembered hand-washing them yesterday. Now they were gone.

"I must be losing my mind," she mumbled to herself.

"Mother, you didn't take my pink bra and undies off the line?" she asked, then chuckled.

Her mother's brow furrowed. "No. I didn't take anything in."

"I didn't think so. They must be in my drawer." She rummaged through her underwear drawer. They weren't there. "Strange." She ran a hand through her silken hair.

Several nights later, in the twilight hours of the evening, she was walking her bullmastiff around the neighborhood, when out of her peripheral vision, she saw a flash of white move behind the garage situated in the middle of the woods, where a neighbor kept his collection of antique cars. She glanced again, and it was gone.

A shiver went up her spine as she quickened her pace. "Let's go home, Houdini," she said to her dog.

She felt completely ill at ease, like she was being watched. "Good thing you look intimidating," she commented to him, who wouldn't hurt anybody. A real gentle giant.

A few days after Kathleen Murphy returned home from Ireland, Olivia popped in to say hello. They got together quite often to have a few glasses of wine and to share lake gossip and engage in fun conversation.

"Welcome home!" she greeted Kathleen, as they shared a friendly hug at the door.

"Thank you! Come on in." Kathleen ushered Olivia in, then headed to the kitchen to pour the Cabernet Sauvignon.

"So how was Ireland?" she inquired as they sat around the cozy fire pit.

"Wonderful," Kathleen enthused, then turned serious. "I should have stayed there."

Olivia laughed, then a quizzical look played on her face. "Why?"

"On top of all the intrigue and mayhem on this lake, now there's a guy running around naked, wearing a Phantom of the Opera mask, peeping into people's windows and shit like that." She disgustedly shook her head as she looked at Olivia's shocked countenance, then continued. "Sometimes he wears a black cape."

"What?" Olivia said derisively. "No way."

Kathleen sipped her wine, then placed it on the patio table. "For real." Her tone was dead serious. "Sylvia Thompson's teenage daughter Sierra was fooling around with her boyfriend in one of the cabins of the YMCA camp when apparently some guy appeared in the doorway, wearing only the mask. He was masturbating watching them. Sierra let out a loud scream — and he took off."

Olivia rolled her eyes. "Sierra? That drama queen? I think she's seen Friday the 13th too many times," she scoffed. "She's always been an attention seeker." She munched on a potato chip. "Me, me, me."

"True," Kathleen concurred. "But she's only the latest victim."

"What?" Olivia listened raptly.

Kathleen gave her a confused look. "You haven't heard?"

"I don't socialize with many people — how would I know this?" She paused, anxiously rubbing her thumb on the wine goblet. "I did take a pontoon boat ride with Angus and your husband — plus a whole bunch of people I didn't know." She smiled. "It was actually entertaining. Good to know everyone on this lake isn't snobby and out to cause you a bunch of shit."

"I know, right?"

Olivia nervously toyed with her hair. "So, what do you mean latest victim?"

"Yeah, some other ladies have reported someone lurking around their house, peering in windows." She held up her finger. "Oh yeah, and lingerie disappearing off their clotheslines."

Olivia's stomach dropped. "Oh my God." She placed a hand over her mouth.

"What?"

"I have been missing some lingerie. I know it was on the line." Her throat went dry, she downed the rest of her wine.

Kathleen's brows shot up. "Oh, no." Her hand quivered slightly as she refilled Olivia's glass. "And my husband is hardly home — only on weekends." She cast a nervous glance at her friend.

Olivia blew out a long breath. "Get some mace. I've had some for years. Luckily, I've never had to use it." She sadly shook her head. "I guess that might change."

Kathleen wearily rubbed her forehead. "Indeed."

Olivia looked pensive. "I wonder if it was one of the guys on that party boat ride I went on." She peered at her friend. "A few were a bit overly friendly."

"Oh?"

"I wasn't going to tell you this, but Dorian Winchester grabbed my butt when I was getting off."

Kathleen chuckled. "Really?"

"Yeah. His wife wasn't on at that point."

"That was still pretty ballsy."

"I thought so." She dipped a chip in the salsa and continued. "Danny Whitcomb was ogling me and chatting me up quite a bit, as well."

Kathleen laughed sarcastically. "With the motley crew of pervs and weirdos on this lake — hell, it could be anybody."

"Sad, but true," Olivia agreed.

They continued to enjoy the evening by the fire, finishing the bottle of wine and talking about lighter topics.

Suddenly, Kathleen's Scottish Terrier started barking and headed towards the arborvitae hedge.

They stared at each other, frantic-looking and wide-eyed.

"What is it, Seamus?" she called to her dog, "good boy."

The two women suspiciously eyed the arborvitae, waiting for some movement.

"I'm calling the police now, you twisted bastard!" Kathleen yelled.

"It was probably a raccoon or opossum," Olivia suggested, her voice a little shaky. "We cranked ourselves up talking about all this shit. Now our imaginations are running wild."

"Probably."

The dog stopped barking and returned to sit by them, still keeping an eye on the arborvitae.

Olivia suddenly remembered the white flash moving behind the neighbor's garage the other night while walking her dog.

She gasped and her face went ashen. "Son of a bitch."

Kathleen whipped her head around. "What now?"

"I — uh ... I just remembered an incident ... the other night." Her voice trembled.

"Oh, Christ!" Kathleen nervously patted her dog. "Do I really want to know?"

Olivia responded tightly, "Probably not ... but I guess you should know." She sighed. "The other night I saw a figure of some sort hiding behind the Cooper's garage ... "

"Shit. So that's probably him out there now." She warily looked around. "The cops are on their way you psycho!" she bellowed again.

Jake Dalton, their next-door neighbor, happened to be on his deck smoking a cigarette. He overheard the commotion.

"Is everything alright over there, ladies?" His voice pierced the silent, inky darkness.

Both women let out a short scream, then realized who it was.

"Jake!" Olivia happily called to him. "Oh my God, what timing!" Her voice was still a little tense. "Could you come over, please? We need a big, strong man."

"On my way!"

Kathleen tugged on Olivia's shirt. "Wait! What if it's him?" she anxiously whispered before he made his way over.

"He's liked me forever, why would he turn into a sicko now, and not 10 years ago?" Olivia laughed. "No way. There's not a snowball's chance in hell that this Doctor Demento running around out there is him," she scoffed. "I've known him his whole life. He has too much character to run around like a weak, pathetic pervert."

Olivia and Jake have a long history. His mother and father moved next door to her when she was around seven. They became best friends with her parents, despite the 20-year age difference – and did everything together. They had a hell of a good time. The neighborhood was actually fun back then, with neighbors constantly in each other's yards, socializing, boating, skinny-dipping.

Olivia's mother would make blueberry muffins every Sunday, and everyone would come and sit around the picnic table and enjoy the food and fellowship.

Sadly, as it happens, Jake's parents divorced when he was a little boy. His father kept the house, while he and his sister moved away with their mom. He would visit his dad, and over the years he developed a crush on Olivia, even though she is 10 years older.

He is now 26, an ex-marine, take-no-bullshit type of dude, working as an auto mechanic.

His father permanently moved to Florida, and he got his house.

They have always had a great friendship, occasionally having a few beers on his porch, even going on a few motorcycle rides. For all these years he has carried a torch for her, wanting to take things to the next level.

Olivia toyed with the idea a few times, but never acted on it. She didn't want to be harassed about being a 'cougar' — even though it's nobody's damned business.

Also, if things went south, being neighbors and having to see each other all the time — things could get bloody awkward! It was flattering and sweet to Olivia to know he still likes her!

"What's going on? Someone harassing you?" he inquired, looking stone-faced, his eyes on Olivia.

"Sit down. Have a beer?" Kathleen gestured toward the fire pit. "We'll fill you in on all the crazy shit going on around here."

After he finished his beer, Olivia decided she should go.

"I have to go check on my mother," she stated seriously.

"I will walk you home," Jake asserted.

She smiled brightly. "Thank you. I would really appreciate that."

They rose to walk home and made sure Kathleen got into her house.

"Lock your doors. Right now," Jake demanded. "If you need anything, let me know."

"I will. Thank you so much. Bye, guys."

On their short walk to Olivia's house, Jake scanned the woods.

"Where are you now, you fucking coward," he loudly announced. "I will tear you a new asshole."

Olivia chuckled.

They reached her doorstep.

"Thank you for escorting me home." She gave him a dazzling smile. "You are awesome." She ran a hand through her hair. "I am really creeped out."

His blue eyes seared into her.

"You know I would snap anyone like a twig if they ever hurt you."

They locked eyes. Olivia felt a surge of warmth shoot through her as she noticed he was getting better-looking with age, as some people do.

"I ... I know!" She quickly averted her gaze and nervously shuffled her feet as they stood very close, face to face.

"I should go in." She didn't want him to think she was leading him on.

"Let me take care of you." He closed in on her and crushed her to him, holding her tightly. "You know I would be good to you — I've always liked you." He rubbed her back. "I don't give a shit about the age difference or anything else." He sighed heavily. "It shouldn't bother you, either."

"I know. I'm sorry. I'm so stressed right now ... about everything." She loosened her grip on him.

"I don't want to let go," he said softly, intensely.

She sensed his passion.

Finally, he let go. "If you ever need help, I will be there, you know that."

"I know. Thank you so much." She turned to open the door. "We'll talk soon, OK?"

"Alright. Goodnight."

"Night."

A few days later she received a phone call from Kathleen. They hadn't gotten together lately because they didn't want Olivia walking home by herself in the dark.

"Hi Kathleen. How is everything?"

"Luckily, I've been fine, no one peeking in on me. And you?"

"Very quiet, thank goodness."

"Nice." The line was quiet for a moment. "Um, unfortunately the Peeping Tom's antics have escalated ... "

Dread shot through Olivia's body. "Oh?" She took a deep breath. "What happened?" She closed her eyes and cringed, waiting for the response.

"Well, Lauren Pearson, a divorced woman in her 60s was recently sexually assaulted. By a guy in a mask."

"So, he's going after old and young. Wonderful. I will have to keep an eye on my mom. Her bedroom is on the first floor, this asshole could climb right in." Olivia rubbed the back of her neck and went on.

"At least I'm on the second floor, he can't climb up onto my balcony without a ladder — and the spiral staircase creaks so much he couldn't sneak up on me."

"Right. Me too, plus I keep my bedroom door locked, and Seamus makes a racket if he hears anything."

"Is Lauren OK?"

"Totally traumatized, obviously. She went out and bought a Doberman Pinscher attack dog."

"Good. Thank God for dogs."

"I know. awesome."

"My dog wouldn't hurt anybody, but does bark and look very intimidating."

Kathleen agreed, "That's true. I got some mace, as well. I keep it next to me in bed."

"Good for you," Olivia sighed. "Too bad it's come to this, eh?"

"I know. Pathetic. We come to the boonies to escape this shit."

"Yep."

"So, how are you and Jake doing?" she probed good-naturedly.

Olivia guffawed. "No news. He walked me home, that's it. We didn't fall into bed."

"Aww — too bad," her friend teased.

"Oh stop!" Olivia rolled her eyes.

"Well, I better clean the house before my husband gets home for the weekend."

"Hey, why don't we all go on the party boat hitch-up this Sunday and see if anyone acts bizarre," she suggested. "Then you and I can compare notes, so to speak." Olivia laughed. "The two of us will suss this whack job out."

"Sounds good. I hope we do. See you Sunday."

"Cool. Bye."

If this warped degenerate comes near my mom, I'll chop his dick off, she thought with a dangerous gleam in her eyes as she put her phone on the counter.

After hearing that distressing news, Olivia decided to sleep on the couch in the living room, right next to her mother's bedroom. If anyone broke in, she'd be right there, mace in hand, and a nice baseball bat to the midsection.

She would ensure her mother's bedroom windows were shut and locked, which might be hard, as her mother always kept the window open for fresh air. Even in the winter, she kept it open a crack. But, safety first, at this point in time. If this lunatic smashed a window, she could rush in.

Olivia settled in for her first night on the couch and it was pretty miserable. So accustomed to her big bed and pitch dark, gloriously silent bedroom, she had a hard time adjusting to the whirring of the refrigerator and the clock chiming every 15 minutes. Plus, her dog came by from time to time to sniff her and stick his face in her face. And the cat slept on top of her.

After a few nights of very little sleep, she wearily made it to the party boat hitch-up on Sunday.

She and her mother, blueberry muffins in hand, joined Derek and Kathleen on their dock, waiting for Angus to pick them up.

They all said their hellos.

"You're looking a little worse for wear," Kathleen remarked to Olivia, taking in her haggard appearance. "No offense."

She smiled wanly. "Thank you. This is taking a toll on me."

Kathleen nodded. "I know. I'm stressed, this is awful."

Angus came around and everyone boarded. They headed to the makeshift bar on the boat. Drinks were made, and they mingled with the people they knew.

They dined on the muffins — and other people provided Danish, croissants, and donuts. It was a great spread. Plus, the Bloody Marys and mimosas flowed freely.

"So, have you noticed anything unusual?" Olivia asked Kathleen quietly as they stood together at the back of one of the boats.

Kathleen scanned the crowd while chewing on a croissant. "Nothing yet." She sipped her mimosa. "No overt leers or flirting ... "

"True. I don't see any guy staring at the women's tits and asses."

Kathleen frowned. "Damn." She glanced over at Tristan Underwood's craft. "I'm surprised he hitched up."

Olivia rolled her eyes. "I know."

Tristan was the richest man on the lake, owning a software company — a multimillionaire.

"He doesn't usually hang out with us riff raff."

Tristan had an elite group of friends on the lake — none as rich as him, although some acted like they were and looked down on the people not in their little clique.

"I don't know why he bothered, they're all just congregating on his boat, as usual."

"Yup. Weird."

The breakfast cruise went on and more libations were quaffed. Some people got boisterous.

Derek was one of them, much to the chagrin of his wife.

Derek, Kathleen, Olivia and Francesca were sitting together chatting amiably, then the topic switched to the naked psycho.

"I hate living like this, I can't sleep, I can't relax, camping out on the couch sucks ... " Olivia shook her head. "I'm sick of this bullshit."

"It's disturbing to live like this," Kathleen commiserated.

Derek decided to say his piece, after a few Bloody Marys, his filter vanished.

"Attention everyone," Derek stated in a loud voice.

The crowd went silent.

"As you probably know, there's some looney toon prowling around the lake, harassing women, watching couples having sex ..."

Kathleen tugged on his shirtsleeve. "Derek! Stop!" she pleaded, her face turning red.

He shrugged her off and continued speaking to the hushed crowd. "If you happen to be on here right now, you twisted son of a bitch, I suggest take your peccadilloes to the Internet ... where there's all kinds of free porn ... "

"Derek!" Kathleen admonished.

"I'm sure every sick fetish could be satisfied on there — and it might save your life ... "

Gasps were heard.

"Because if I catch you on my property, peeking in my windows — I will blow your goddamned head off," he bluntly stated.

Kathleen anxiously rubbed her forehead as Derek stopped his tirade and sat down. "Can you drop us off please?" she sweetly requested to Angus, embarrassed to death.

Olivia scanned the faces of the crowd. No one looked guilty or nervous. Some look bemused, others confused, and some people thoroughly got a kick out of his drunken rant.

The boat dropped them off at the Murphy's dock.

"Did you have to go into your little harangue?" Kathleen chastised Derek, who had a little buzz going.

He gave her an annoyed look. "I thought you'd appreciate that. I'm trying to protect you."

Olivia stood up for him, "I agree. Maybe he will stay away from us. It also gave me a chance to eyeball the crowd for a reaction." She frowned. "Unfortunately, no one looked peculiar or shifty listening to Derek."

Kathleen calmed down. "You're right." She rubbed her husband's shoulder. "I'm sorry, honey."

He gave her a soft smile, "I know. We're all on edge."

Everyone said their farewells and Francesca and Olivia walked home. Olivia, being exhausted from her sleepless, stress-filled nights, went home and took a nap.

Over a week went by and Olivia was still sleeping on the couch. She was cranky and ready to move far away from this wretched lake. She thought that perhaps the psycho was on the party boat that day and Derek's blunt speech got through to him.

No such luck.

It was a Wednesday, around 2:10 in the morning, when she was actually dead asleep on the couch, utterly exhausted from the constant worry and strain, when her cat's head shot up and she peered towards the sliding glass door. Seeing that the cat slept on top of her, the movement jolted her awake.

She was bone-tired but instantly alert. She broke out in a cold sweat as she looked into the inky darkness.

The sliding glass door was open only a little way, not enough for anybody to squeeze through, but enough to allow some fresh air in. And it helped to hear any noise outside.

Lucky for her, the cat also picked up on movement and sounds.

Thank you, Spartacus! she thought.

She had wedged a board behind the door, so it couldn't be opened any wider.

The curtain was shut, so no one could see in, but the moonlight illuminated a figure standing there.

The outline of the cape with silhouetted.

Olivia's blood ran cold and she resisted the urge to let out a shriek.

She thought about running to her mother's room, bolting the door, keeping her mace at the ready, and letting the cops handle it.

No, I have to do this, I have to finish this chaos now, she told herself determinedly.

She was shaking like a leaf as she silently, furtively crept off the couch and over to the sliding glass door, mace in hand.

She took a deep breath, trying to muster up the strength to face the intruder.

Can I really do this?

She heard the screen being cut with a knife, of course he didn't know the door itself wouldn't open any farther, being stopped by a board. Before he got that far, Olivia sprang into action.

This is it.

Standing silently behind the curtain, she threw it open and aimed the mace at his face and mouth, hoping the noxious stuff would penetrate through that eerie, ghoulish Phantom of the Opera mask.

Without making a sound, she sprayed through the screen, having the element of surprise on her side.

She heard him gagging and gasping.

"My eyes!" he yelled as he stumbled back and away from the door.

"You sick son of a bitch!" she yelled.

She quickly removed the board from the door and in a flash opened the screen door and went out onto the deck in an instant, her adrenaline pumping like mad. She didn't want the confrontation in the house, or want her beloved dog coming out onto the deck and getting stabbed.

She slammed the screen door. Her dog at that point had bolted from her mother's room where he slept. He was woofing behind the screen door.

The board from the door was in her hand.

The psycho had stumbled backwards blindingly, and now was pinned up against the railing, moaning in agony from the poison.

"You're lucky I don't chop your dick off!" Olivia bellowed.

She swung the board hard at his midsection and heard a crack as he fell to the floor, writhing in pain.

The dog kept woofing at the door.

"Good boy, Houdini."

Suddenly, another figure appeared out of the night and bounded onto the deck.

"Oh my God! What the hell is going on!" she screamed as she readied the board to swing at the second figure, her eyes wild.

"Olivia! It's me! Jake!"

"Jake! Holy shit!" She dropped the board and they ran to each other.

She sobbed uncontrollably.

"I came to help you, but you look like you did a good job yourself." He chuckled as he caressed her hair and soothed her.

"No, I'm so glad you came!" She hugged him tighter.

"You know I would kill anyone who ever hurt you — or tried to," he vowed.

The deck light came on. Olivia's mom appeared at the door, wide-eyed with fright.

"Is everything OK?" she asked in a shaky voice as she stood by the barking dog.

Olivia glanced at her. "Mother! It's alright, stay there."

The light illuminated the pervert still writhing on the deck.

It was a bizarre scene, a naked man clad in a cape and Phantom of the Opera mask moaning and groaning.

Jake broke away from Olivia to confront the man.

"You sick bastard." He gave him a few swift kicks to his gut, resisting the urge to finish him off.

The man was gasping. "I can't breathe."

"Good. I hope you die," Jake bit out. He reached down and flung off the mask.

It was Olivia's turn to gasp. "Oh my God. No way ... "

"Call the cops," she told her mother.

It wasn't one of the flirty, grabby men on the boat that night — it was Tristan Underwood, the multi-millionaire who lives 5 houses down from them.

Francesca put a hand to her mouth. "I don't believe it."

Jake disgustedly shook his head. "Why would you fuck up your perfect life to do this shit like this?"

He got no response.

Jake stayed to comfort the women until the cops showed up and hauled Tristan away.

Then they all shared a vodka tonic around the patio table.

"I can't thank you enough, Jake." Francesca's mom beamed at him.

Olivia gazed at him warmly. "How did you know?"

He locked eyes with her. "I heard the dog woofing and you screaming ... " He caressed her hand and continued, "I told you I would never let anyone hurt you."

She flashed her sweet smile and kissed his cheek. "Thank you."

Olivia and Jake became a couple soon after that. They were also sick of the neighborhood bullshit, lack of privacy, the snobby assholes, and all the rest of the pandemonium around them.

They sold their houses and bought a beautiful hip roof colonial in the woods of Maine, with acres of land. Not a neighbor in sight! Paradise!

Her mom moved into the attached in-law apartment, and everyone was incredibly happy, leaving the insanity and intrigue of Blue Lake, now known as Scandal Lake, far, far behind.

About the Authors

Beth Liberty is a previously published author. Her first novel is 'Just Remember I Love You.'

Adrienne Smyth is a published author in many scientific journals. This is her first piece of fictional writing. She is presently a part-time Biology professor.